**What Others Are Sa**
*This Doesn't Happen in the Mo*

## 5 Star Review!

There is little doubt that Renée Pawlish is a promising new voice to the comic murder/mystery genre. Quite noticeable...is Pawlish's adept development of the plot coupled with her ability to contrive clear, concise and playful prose with almost perfect pacing.

Norman Goldman, Bookpleasures Publisher and Editor
Top Amazon Reviewer

## Sam Spade Eat Your Heart Out

I laughed, I cringed and I enjoyed this fast-paced mystery. I look forward to reading more about Reed Ferguson's shenanigans in the future.

The Book Diva Reviews

## What Others Are Saying About
### *Nephilim Genesis of Evil* by Renée Pawlish

## 5 Star Review

Stephen King and Dean Koontz have long been known as masters of horror. I believe you can add Renee Pawlish to that list... The plot is entrancing. It grabbed my attention from the beginning and held it to the end.

Readers' Favorite

## A Spooky Blend of Biblical Intrigue and Modern Paranormal

This book is clearly written by a pro. The scenes are colored with rich description, depth of character and a cast that is reminiscent of Henry Fonda's *On Golden Pond*. However, there is an evil in this story that FINALLY brings the Nephilim to life and uncovers the dark secrets that scripture has keep hidden for millennium. If you enjoy reading supernatural fiction that meshes our distant past and the present, you will enjoy this most excellent book.

Kindle Book Review

# Reel Estate Rip-off

## A Reed Ferguson Mystery

Copyright 2011 by Renée Pawlish
Cover Design copyright by Ryan Bibby

This book is a work of fiction. Names, characters, places, and incidents are
either products of the author's imagination or used fictitiously. Any resemblance
to actual events, locales, or persons, living or dead, is entirely coincidental. All
rights reserved. No part of this publication can be reproduced or transmitted in
any form or by any means, electronic or mechanical, without permission in
writing from Renée Pawlish.

December 2011

# ACKNOWLEDGEMENTS

The author gratefully acknowledges all those who helped in the writing of this book, especially: Beth Hecker, Beth Treat, Terri Pavalko, and my parents. If I've forgotten anyone, please accept my apologies.

# CHAPTER ONE

"Arnold Schwarzenegger is the greatest actor ever!"

Ace Smith stood just inside the doorway of my office, glaring at his brother, Deuce. The opening shot of a long-standing argument between the Goofball Brothers had been delivered.

"Dude, Sly is way better." Deuce's lips curled in a half-grin at his older brother. Then Deuce gestured for me to hurry up.

"Bruce Willis is better than Sly." Ace grabbed a pen from my desk and began waving it like a sword. He had a triumphant look on his baby face.

"He doesn't even do action movies," Deuce said, rolling his eyes.

"Hello! Can you say *Die Hard*? One of the best pictures ever," Ace said.

"Better than *The Terminator*? No way!" Deuce advanced into the room, snatched a pencil off the desk, and held it up.

"Hold on." Ace spread his arms like a referee keeping two boxers, or in this case, jousters, apart. "Let's ask Reed. He's knows movies. And he's a detective."

I turned my head in surprise. It was true. I was a movie buff. And a detective. But I had been sitting at my desk, trying to ignore the interchange while listening to a voice mail message. I didn't want to get involved.

"Yeah, Reed. What do you think?" Deuce asked.

No one ever won this argument, which was why it still continued. I hung up the phone, and shrugged my shoulders to indicate my indifference. I didn't care. "You know what my vote is."

"Oh yeah. Henry Bogart," Ace said, pointing the pen at me. "All that *film now* stuff. That Bogart guy is dead, you know, so that doesn't count."

"It's *Humphrey* Bogart and *film noir*," I corrected him with a laugh, pointing at a framed Bogart movie poster of *The Big Sleep* on the wall. "And Bogie can act circles around any of your guys." I pocketed my keys and led them out to the small waiting room.

"Talking golf again," Deuce joked. They both laughed. It was a hot, dry Friday afternoon in August. The temperature in downtown Denver was hovering in the mid-90's, perfect conditions for a few cold ones during happy hour. I had decided to call it a day early and had phoned the brothers, who were available at that time of day because they were ending a week of vacation. Now we were heading over to B 52's, a local pool hall, and I was heading into the weekend. No work until Monday. Actually, I'd wrapped up a case a week ago, and hadn't done much since. Famous last words.

I shooed the brothers out the door and was locking it behind me when I heard another voice, distinctly un-Goofball-like.

"Reed Ferguson?" Each word was enunciated carefully, a clipped tone.

I turned. The ghost of Burt Lancaster gazed back at me. "Swede?"

"Excuse me?" A confused expression spread across the man's face. Okay, not slick on my part, but he was the spitting image of Lancaster in his film debut as Swede Andersen in *The Killers*, a classic noir film. Same face, same perfectly coiffed dark hair with the wavy curls, same dark, chilling eyes. Except that Swede Andersen wouldn't be wearing a three-piece suit and Gucci loafers. And right now the eyes were dimmed by a look of sadness.

"Has anyone ever told you you look like Burt Lancaster?"

The confused look on his face vanished, replaced by annoyance. "A time or two," he said, his jaw tightening.

"Never mind," I said. Behind him, the Goofball Brothers stared at me impatiently, shifting around like two little boys who needed to pee really badly. "I'm Reed."

He shook my hand firmly, all business. "Jack Healy. I've caught you at a bad time," he said by way of an apology, though I detected no hint of sorrow in his voice.

I gestured toward the guys. "We were heading out, but I can spare you a few minutes." Behind Jack Healy, Ace started waving his hands in a "no way" gesture, while Deuce looked crestfallen. They had already been antsy to leave. Was I going to have the nerve to ask them to wait longer?

"Why don't you guys go on, and I'll catch up with you later." I may be crazy, but I wasn't stupid. If I had the brothers wait in my office, within two minutes they'd be arguing and fighting like ten-year-olds. *That* would make a good impression on a prospective client.

They both relaxed visibly, goofy smiles on their goofy faces. "We'll see you there," Ace called as they hurried off down the hall.

"Thank you," Jack said, throwing a hesitant look at the retreating brothers.

I opened the door and escorted Jack into the inner office. He took a seat across from my desk and waited until I had settled into a chair, my elbows leaning on the desk, giving him the best attention I could muster for a Friday afternoon right before happy hour.

"I'm sorry to bother you right before the weekend," he began. And again, I didn't think he sounded sorry at all. He looked more irritated, like he thought I shouldn't be leaving my office before five o'clock. If he only knew the erratic hours I kept. Ah, the life of a detective. "I took off work early to swing by your office, so I really wanted to be sure I saw you today," Jack continued. "I can't afford to take the time at all, but it seems necessary." He hesitated, glanced at his watch, then back at me. "I want to hire you."

Obviously, considering he was here, I chose to think.

Jack paused to gather his thoughts. Then he leaned forward in the chair. "I want to hire you to find my brother's killer. Or killers."

I stared back at him. "You've got my attention."

His gaze seemed to say, "About time." "I suppose I should start at the beginning," was what he did say.

"That would be good."

And so he did, loosening his tie as he talked. "My brother Ned was killed a month ago. He fell while cycling in the mountains. We think he lost control of his bike and ended up over the side of a cliff." I vaguely remembered seeing something about that on the news, but kept silent. Jack sighed. "He broke his neck in the fall and was killed instantly." A pained look crossed his face, and he stopped.

I waited a beat before saying, "I don't understand. How could there be a killer or killers if your brother fell? It sounds more like a terrible accident."

"I don't believe it happened that way." Jack glared at me with grim determination. "The police ruled it an accident. The autopsy indicated that Ned was drunk and on barbiturates and didn't know what he was doing, but I know better."

"How?"

"First of all, Ned didn't drink much, and he didn't do drugs. And he never went cycling. He hated being in the mountains, hated driving on the winding roads. He wouldn't have gone up there, and certainly not when he was drunk."

"Where did this happen?"

"Outside of Buena Vista. There's a trail that runs near Mount Princeton. They found his car parked at a trail head. He died on a Saturday but his body wasn't found for three days. There's no way anyone will convince me that he went there alone, or willingly. Not Ned."

I contemplated Jack's straightforward gaze. He seemed sure about what he was saying. "How can you be so certain that your brother wouldn't go cycling, or that he could fall while doing it? That could happen to any of us."

"Ned was afraid of heights. Pathologically afraid. He never went cycling, hiking, climbing, or anything like that in the mountains. He wouldn't even sit by a window in a high-rise building."

This piqued my interest. "The police checked into this, right?"

He nodded, chewing at his lower lip. "Sure. But everything pointed to it being ruled exactly like they said. There wasn't a shred of evidence to make them think differently."

"Did you tell them your suspicions?"

"Yes. But with the evidence they had, they said they concluded that accidents happen." He picked at the perfect crease in his trousers as he talked. "They dropped it. But I know it couldn't have happened that way. If I have to pay someone myself to find out the truth, I'll do it." He stopped with the pant leg and looked up at me. "Are you willing to find out what happened to my brother?"

I did a quick mental inventory of my schedule in my head. Nothing coming up. Last case finished a week ago. I'd spent more time playing pool in the last seven days than I had in months, and my game still wasn't very good. I'd never solve the Best Actor argument with the Goofball Brothers. "I'll take it," I said.

"Sounds good." Sounding just like Burt Lancaster.

# CHAPTER TWO

The goldfish looked hungry.

That was the first thing I thought as I followed Jack Healy into the living room of his brother Ned's house in Commerce City. Maybe it was the way the little guy was gaping at me, with his big black eyes, and his mouth puffing out like he wanted someone to put something in it. He swam around the rectangular tank, gazed at me with big, sad eyes, swam, then turned back to me. What a life.

Ned had been in dire financial straits.

That was the second thing I thought as I turned from the fish tank to survey the rest of the room. There were exactly two pieces of furniture in the room. The fish tank, sitting on a stack of cinder blocks, if you could call that furniture, and opposite the tank, a threadbare couch that literally leaned on three legs.

Jack had signed a standard contract and paid my retainer fee last night, but by that time he was already late for a dinner appointment, so we decided to meet at Ned's house today. I needed more than Jack's gut feeling to determine if Ned had really been murdered. Maybe Ned's house would tell me something.

"The house is exactly as Ned left it?" I asked. Maybe Ned killed himself because he didn't have anything, like furniture and decorations, I thought wryly.

Jack nodded. "I've been through his bills, that's it."

My eyes darted around the bare room and blank walls. "Why would someone want to kill your brother?" I asked, avoiding the couch as if it might have fleas.

Jack shrugged his shoulders as he focused on the fish, tapping out a generous serving of food from a tiny canister on the tank stand. "I've racked my brain trying to answer that one. That's another reason why the police don't think Ned was murdered: there's no motive." The fish gulped at the food with a vengeance.

"Did he have any enemies? Any trouble with the law?"

"No and no." Jack screwed the lid back on the fish food, and turned back to face me. "Ned was just an ordinary guy. I've looked over his financial statements, checked his bills and mail. Nothing stands out."

I gestured around the room. "By the looks of it, he didn't have much money."

Jack sighed. "That wasn't always the case. Ned was a realtor, he sold houses. He did quite well for himself."

"What happened? This isn't the home of a wealthy man."

"He made a lot from the huge boom in housing sales and values," Jack said. Denver was on the A-list for many people in the latter part of the 1990's, which helped cause a huge rise in the housing market. "Ned had a great life. At least until recently." Jack rubbed a hand over his face, as if trying to wipe away bad memories. "Everything seemed to be going fine. He had a beautiful wife, a big house, not like this old place. He had nice cars, took great vacations. He had the dream life. Then it all went south."

That explained the house we were in. "What happened?"

Jack moved as if he was going to sit on the couch, but thought better of it. He motioned for me to follow him into the kitchen. It was tiny, with barely enough room for one person. The cabinets were stained a seventies dark brown, and the appliances carried on the theme, all of which was once fashionably called gold. The walls were grayish white. Nothing hung on them, but you could make out lighter spots where decorations had once hung. Jack crossed to a miniscule table in the corner of the room and sat down on a rolling chair next to it.

"I'm not sure what happened," Jack began. "No, that's not true. I know what happened, he lost it all. I just don't know all the whys. Ned and I didn't talk a lot about our work."

I opened the refrigerator door. A can of Pepsi, an opened box of Arm & Hammer baking soda, and a jug of water. "Did you clean this out?"

Jack shook his head. "That's all there was. There are a few frozen dinners in the freezer. I need to go through the house and clean it out, but I haven't felt like it."

"What do you do?" I checked the cabinets while he talked, but other than a few dry goods and some mismatched dishes, they were bare.

"I own a computer consulting firm. We do all kinds of programming, all over the United States." He crossed his hands, resting them on the table. "It has very little to do with real estate, so there wasn't a lot of common ground between Ned and me. And we didn't talk as much anymore."

"What about things not related to work?" I sat down on a chair opposite him. "Did you talk about other stuff?"

"No, and I'll regret that until the day I die." Jack stared at his hands for a moment. "We used to be closer."

"Then how can you be sure that he wouldn't have gone cycling?"

He planted a firm gaze on me. "I may not have known everything that happened in his life, but I know Ned wouldn't go cycling in the mountains. That would've meant Ned conquered his fear of heights, and I can't imagine that he wouldn't mention that."

"Why weren't you close?"

"He married Samantha." Jack said her name like it was a four-letter-word. "We, my wife and I, were never fond of Samantha." The same vile sound to the name. "Fond" was definitely an understatement.

"How long were they married?"

"Two years." Jack exhaled noisily. "Two years too long."

"What's Samantha like?" I asked, bracing myself for the negative vibes.

"She wasn't nice, I can tell you that. Samantha is the most self-absorbed, possessive, ruthless, and greedy person I've ever met. She set her sights on Ned and wouldn't be denied. When he met her, he was making money hand over fist, and she decided she was going to partake of it. By the time she got her hooks out of him, she'd taken every dime from him."

I scooted my chair back a bit, away from his intensity. "Ned didn't notice that she was bad news?"

Jack stood up and stared out the sliding glass doors onto a weed-choked lawn the size of a cardboard box. "He was in love. Or lust." He emitted a rasping laugh. "That was my take on it. Samantha was a looker, no doubt. It wasn't like she was a model or anything. But Ned fell for her." He whirled away from the window. "Let me show you a picture of her."

I followed Jack down a short hallway to a room that was designed to be a small bedroom, but had been converted into an office. A paint-splattered, worn oak desk sat against one wall, with an older model Dell computer and monitor on it. A beat-up metal file cabinet stood to the left of the desk. Jack opened the bottom file drawer and pulled out a snapshot.

"I don't know why he kept it, but I found it when I was going through his bills." He handed the photo to me.

Samantha was pretty, but not quite perfect enough to be considered beautiful. Her brown eyes seemed just a bit cold, her long blond hair was cut a little too plain, and her nose was maybe just a bit too big. But she had full lips that pursed into just the right kind of sexy pout. She had her arms crossed over large breasts, and gold jewelry glinted from her wrists. A huge diamond ring rested on her left ring finger. "She is a looker," I repeated Jack's description.

"Don't let that fool you," Jack said, putting the picture back. "She was nothing short of a bitch." At least he was honest.

"Maybe she wanted him dead," I said, reaching for a motive.

"Maybe," Jack agreed. "By the time they divorced, she hated him, and she was mean enough to want him dead."

"Did Ned owe her any money?"

"Not that I know of. She gets his inheritance, but that isn't much."

"Why didn't he change his will? Why let her inherit?"

Jack shrugged. "I don't know."

"How much will she inherit?" Never underestimate the power of money. What seems like a little to one person is a fortune for another.

"A few thousand dollars is all." Scratch that motive, I thought. Jack grimaced. "She had more to gain with Ned alive, believe me. Samantha was getting hefty alimony checks. That's part of what finally broke Ned, having to pay her each month."

"But that alone couldn't have left him with nothing. What else led to his financial downfall?" I asked.

"Ned didn't tell me a lot, but I know that he bought a lot of real estate in some other states, speculating that the values would rise like they have here in Colorado. It didn't turn out that way, though, and Ned wasn't able to pay some of his creditors. He had to file for bankruptcy, and then his house sales tumbled. I thought he had things under control, but apparently not. Once he was headed toward financial ruin, Samantha left him. But that didn't stop her from gouging him. She got the house in the divorce settlement, and alimony." Jack waved his hand in the air. "Ned could barely afford this." He paused, contemplating the sparse surroundings. "Ned was a smart guy, and I just don't understand how he could let all this happen to him."

I could see how his bewilderment would make him want to find a reason for Ned's death. But I wasn't finding much to convince me that Ned had been murdered. "Mind if I glance through his records?" I asked.

"Help yourself." Jack stepped aside and stood leaning against the wall while I perused Ned's files. With the exception of his real estate files, his records were as bare as the house. The top two drawers were crammed with real estate contracts and other paperwork, going back a number of years.

"Why doesn't Ned keep all this on the computer?" I asked.

Jack shrugged. "He was working in that direction, but he was a bit old-school and liked to have hard copies as well."

After glancing at a few of them I moved to the bottom drawer, where Jack had retrieved the picture of Samantha. I found a few credit card statements, all close to maxed out, an electric bill that was two months behind, and a phone bill, also past due. And the picture of Samantha.

"He was in a lot of debt," I said.

"Like I said, it was tough for him lately."

"Anything in the closet?" I pointed at folding doors on the opposite wall.

"It's empty," Jack said as I opened it. Not a thing in it – except dust.

"How about the rest of the house?"

"Come with me." Jack led the way into the only other bedroom in the house. It was slightly bigger than the office, with a tiny bathroom with a shower stall off one side. I opened the medicine cabinet over the sink. It contained a number of toiletries, but no prescription drugs of any kind. I didn't see any indication of drugs in the rest of the bathroom either.

I searched the bedroom next. A mattress on a box spring was centered on one wall under a window, with threadbare blue sheets covering it. By their rumpled appearance, I assumed that making the bed had not been a priority for Ned. A phone and a small brass lamp stood on the floor beside the bed. Stacks of T-shirts, blue jeans, socks, and underwear lay against the wall by the door to the bathroom. I noticed nothing unusual, unless you categorized not having a dresser as odd. But what did catch my eye was a poster on the wall above the clothes.

I took a good look. "Ned liked old movies?" I asked.

The poster was an advertisement from the movie *The Maltese Falcon*, with Humphrey Bogart and Mary Astor. A classic movie, one of my favorites, with my favorite actor. Bogie – the man, the detective. On my better days, I liked to think I was as good as he was. It rarely happened, which says something of my amateur skills.

The poster wasn't in great shape, somewhat faded with some wrinkles on the paper, and a few small tears in it. But for a movie buff like me, it was like gazing at a Picasso.

"I don't think so," Jack said, barely giving it attention.

"You know, an original can cost a fortune these days, depending on how rare the poster is and what condition it's in. There's a huge market in old Hollywood memorabilia."

Jack nodded, but based off the bored look on his face he'd already lost interest in what I was saying. "Maybe he was trying for a new style after his divorce." He headed for the door. "That certainly wasn't Samantha's taste."

"It's good taste," I said, showing my bias. I had a similar poster hanging in my office. An original. And it was expensive, upwards of ten thousand dollars. I hadn't paid that much for it, but enough that it was an extravagance. I had to buy it – it was Bogie.

"You might as well see the rest of the house, although I don't know what you'll find." Jack stalked back down the hallway. I took one last longing look at the poster before I dashed after him.

The remainder of the house consisted of a pint-sized unfinished basement, and a one-car garage, with a beat-up Honda Civic parked in the available space. Two hooks penetrated the cross beams above the hood of the car, where a bike would've been stored. I pointed to them.

"Are you sure Ned didn't ride?"

Jack studied them. "I guess he could've. I've never heard him talk about it. But he probably would've owned a road bike, not a mountain bike."

"Did they find a road bike with his body?"

Jack scowled. "It was a mountain bike." He kept looking at the hooks. "I don't understand. Ned never said anything about taking up cycling, either road or mountain riding."

"People change," I said.

While Jack continued to muse about Ned, I carefully rummaged through the ten-gallon trashcan in the corner and found some old newspapers and more than a dozen frozen dinner boxes. And plenty of Pepsi cans. I guess Ned didn't believe in recycling. But if he was a drinker, or if he used drugs, I didn't find any evidence in his house. And I also found absolutely nothing that would indicate that he had met his end through foul play, and I told Jack this.

"My money's good," he said, determination etched in his tense jaw lines. "I may not have been close to Ned recently, but I'm still his brother, and I know he wouldn't go riding in the mountains like that, alone or with someone. Even if that's there." He jabbed a finger at the hooks. "I need to know what really happened. Otherwise I'll always have questions." A guilty tone crept into his voice, and I wondered what brought it out. The lost connection with his brother, or something else?

"Where does Samantha live?" Maybe Ned's former wife could shed some light on his untimely death. "I'll have a talk with her."

"In Highlands Ranch," Jack said, naming a sprawling community of newer homes in south-suburban Denver. "She still lives in the house they bought after they were married." We traipsed back through the tiny kitchen and into the living room. "Watch yourself. She's brutal. Samantha took everything from Ned."

Not everything, I thought ruefully, as I eyed the little goldfish swimming contentedly in his tank.

# CHAPTER THREE

Samantha Healy lived in one of the newer neighborhoods in suburban Highlands Ranch. I wasn't particularly fond of the area – too many houses that followed a few basic floor plans. The homes were all two-story with three-car garages and vaulted roofs, each at least three thousand square feet, and every house was painted a neutral shade of tan with off-white trim. Where was the originality? As I drove along a wide street I couldn't help but feel that the area lacked the kind of charm that older neighborhoods have.

After getting Samantha Healy's phone number from Jack, I had spent the entire weekend trying to get in touch with her. I got an answering machine each time I called, and concluded, as a shrewd detective would, that she was either screening her calls, or she wasn't home. So on Monday morning, I decided to visit her personally.

I pulled the 4-runner up in front of a house with a number of windows in the front, and a porch just large enough to display a green Welcome mat at the door. I rang the bell and waited, peeking in through the beveled glass window beside the door. After a moment, I heard the sharp click of heels and a shadow approached. Then the door opened.

I was speechless for a moment. The person before me was Samantha, but at the same time it wasn't. This woman had the same face, the same build, the same breasts, but angry lines spread around eyes that stared at me with an intense fury. Her lips turned down into a scowl and I prepared for her to bite at me.

"What do you want?" she snapped.

"Samantha?" I asked, taken aback. Perhaps she'd forgotten about the Welcome sign I was standing on.

"Yes? What do you want?" she repeated, clearly irate.

I introduced myself. "I'd like to speak to you about Ned Healy."

If she was trying to look even angrier, she succeeded. I didn't know eyebrows could actually join together until I saw hers do just that. Then she slammed the door shut. And I did what every detective in every pulp novel or movie did. I stuck my size-ten Reebok in the entryway to block the door from closing. And I damn near screamed as the heavy wood crushed my foot into the doorjamb. Those fictional detectives who managed this trick in so smooth and suave a manner must never have actually tried it.

"Argh," I grunted, putting my hands on the door and pushing back. Maybe if I wore a Fedora like Bogie I'd look tough enough that I wouldn't have to go through this. I pushed harder.

I swear Samantha snarled as she pushed with equal force on the other side of the door, surprising me with her strength. I heaved my shoulder into the door and shoved. "Look," I gasped. "I just need a few moments of your time. I'm not the police."

She suddenly stepped back and I catapulted into the entryway, stumbling and then catching myself on a half-table across from the door. I righted myself and turned around. I felt just like a cat that, misjudging a jump and falling ungracefully to the floor, looks at you like "I meant to do that."

"Are you always this nice to visitors?" I asked, resisting an urge to take my shoe off and rub my wounded foot.

"You're not a visitor," she said, snipping off each word as if she were breaking twigs. "More like an intruder." She crossed her arms and glared at me. "You have one minute to explain yourself, or I'm calling the police." To emphasize her threat, she pulled a tiny cell phone from her jeans pocket and prepared to dial.

"I was hired by Jack Healy. He doesn't believe that Ned's death was an accident."

"Oh, brother," Samantha said, rolling her eyes in an exaggerated manner. "Now I've heard it all. I should call the psych ward, not the police."

"Why do you say that?" I took a more imposing position with both feet firmly planted on the floor. She'd need a crane to move me. Or the cops.

"It was an accident, you idiot. The police said so. He ran his bike off the trail."

"Did Ned like to ride when you were married?"

"Ride what?" she snapped.

"A bicycle."

She hesitated. "No, but maybe he'd taken it up in the last year. The man needed something cheap to do, that's for sure. But my money says he set this whole thing up himself."

"What do you mean?"

Samantha leaned forward as if she was telling me a secret. "If you want my opinion, Ned committed suicide and made it look like an accident."

"That doesn't make sense."

"Ned was not a sensible man."

"How can you be so certain he committed suicide?"

"Have you seen where he lives? The car he drives?" Samantha threw her hands up. "The man doesn't *have* anything. A few pieces of furniture and bare walls that a stupid movie poster won't help. He screwed up and lost everything. And he couldn't live with that."

Wow. The words "amicable divorce" definitely did not apply.

"Did he ever seem suicidal when you were still married? Or depressed?"

"Are you listening to me? He was depressed all the time. He hated his life, what he turned into. The fact that he'd lost everything."

"Why make it look like an accident unless someone was going to benefit?"

"You mean insurance money?"

I nodded. "But who would get the insurance money? You?"

Samantha briefly considered this. "Of course not. Maybe he was thinking about his brother." The silence stretched out. "You're the detective," she said at last, unable to defend her theory. "You figure it out."

"That's what I'm trying to do," I hit back. "Did he drink a lot or do any drugs?"

"Ned never took any drugs, and he only drank a little. Although the last time we talked, he sounded drunk."

"When was that?"

She screwed up her face, thinking. It was not a becoming look for her. "I think it was a couple of weeks before he died. He kept talking about how things were going to turn around, that I'd see a different Ned. Like I haven't heard that before. The man didn't have a dime, so how was he going to turn things around?"

"What about the alimony he paid you?"

"What about it?"

"Might that have something to do with his having no money?"

For a second I thought she might smack me, but instead she chose to bore a hole into me with her eyes. "I gave up a promising career when I married Ned. He at least owed me for that."

"And what career was that?" I asked.

"I'm an actress," she said, tossing her hair in a not-too-subtle eye-catching way. I tried to keep the corners of my mouth from moving up, but she must've seen something in my expression. "It's true." Now she pulled some hair behind her ears. "I've done some theater, and commercials. And I was in line for a new Steven Spielberg movie, but then Ned swept me off my feet."

This version definitely didn't fit with what Jack had told me. "Really?" I wasn't sure what else to say.

"It's true." She flicked her hair again. "As you can see, I would've made a lot of money if I had continued my career. I felt Ned owed me for that. Once I got some good acting jobs, I was going to revisit the alimony."

"What are you going to do now?"

She started to answer, then stopped. "I can't see that that's any of your business. And I said I'd give you a minute, which I did. Your time's up."

I wondered what had made her end the conversation so abruptly. "Here's my card." I pulled one out of my wallet. "If you can think of anything that might be helpful, please call me."

"Anything helpful about a suicide?" she said with more than a hint of sarcasm, taking my card and dropping it unceremoniously on the half-table.

"If it was suicide." I stepped cautiously by her and out the door. It slammed with a thunk behind me.

## CHAPTER FOUR

I left Samantha's house and drove back downtown, mulling over my not-so-pleasant conversation with her. Either Samantha had changed after Ned divorced her, or he had definitely been blinded by love because I couldn't see how Samantha's personality would woo anyone.

I spent the remainder of the day preparing a file for the Jack Healy case, paying some bills, working out, and practicing at the gun range. Last Christmas, while working on my first case, I'd been shot in the rear. The embarrassing incident made me acutely aware of how vulnerable I'd been, so I felt it would be prudent if I bought a gun. Bogie had a gun, I rationalized. Having bought one, I felt it would be even better if I knew how to use it.

When I finished at the practice range, I took the gun back to my office and placed it back in a locked box on a high shelf in the closet. Hey, I didn't say I was ready to actually carry it around yet. My errands done, I decided to head home.

I own a third-story condo in the Uptown neighborhood east of downtown. Since the Goofball Brothers, who were anything but party animals, lived below me and we were the only tenants in the newly constructed building, living here was peaceful.

I parked in the alley garage and walked around the side of the house to the stairs that led up to my place.

"Hey, stranger," I heard a sultry voice call out.

"Hey, yourself." I turned to see Willie Rhoden walking over to me.

"You're just getting home?" I nodded. "Have you eaten? We could order a pizza or Chinese."

I smiled. Willie, real name Wilhelmina, was my neighbor, and I'd had a crush on her since she moved into the building across the street a year ago. She had recently broken up with her longtime boyfriend, Alan, and I had tried more than once to get Willie to go out on a date with me, only to be politely rebuffed. I assumed that she needed time to get over Alan.

"Dinner sounds great," I said. "My treat?" Willie was an emergency room admissions nurse at nearby St. Joseph's hospital, and I was so enamored of her that I thought her petite frame looked great in her medical smock. Even her sturdy walking shoes gave her just the right amount of boost to her height. She tucked her short blond hair behind her ears, her mischievous green eyes twinkling.

"No, we split the cost." Willie linked her arm in mine and I could smell jasmine in her hair. "That way things don't get complicated."

"How is my paying for dinner complicated?" I asked as we strolled across the street to her building.

"Are you working on a new case?" she changed the subject.

"Just started something. I'm not sure where this one is going yet."

"I hope you'll be careful. I'd hate to see you get shot again."

I laughed, but her emerald eyes sliced through me. "I'm sure this isn't as dangerous."

Willie stopped at the door. "Reed, I like you. A lot. Even before I broke up with Alan, I was tempted to go out with you. But you want to know why I won't?"

"Because you need time to get over Alan?"

She shook her head. "That's only part of the reason. I don't want to get involved with you and then find out that you've been hurt or killed."

If she'd thrown ice water in my face, I wouldn't have been more surprised. I forced another laugh. "C'mon. I got shot in the rear as I was diving to the floor. An inch higher and the bullet would've gone right over me." An inch in another direction, and I might not be able to have kids, but I didn't think Willie would appreciate the humor, so I left it unsaid.

"But it could've gone any number of ways," Willie pointed out. "I've seen it happen before. You were lucky it was only your ass."

"And what a cute ass it is." I grinned at her.

Willie stared at me, her cute lips turning into a frown.

"You also were attacked right here on the street," she said, referring to the same case, in which a bat-wielding female vigilante assaulted me on the sidewalk outside my building.

"And I lived through it." I beamed at her. "Besides, you even helped me out on that case. Why did you do that if you're so concerned about me?" Willie had helped with a deception by pretending to be my client and luring the FBI after her so my client and I could get to a rendezvous undetected.

"I thought that it would be fun. And it was. But it never seemed dangerous." She paused, biting her lip. "I know that sounds naïve, but it seemed harmless at the time. Then when you got shot, the reality of what you do for a living hit me."

We lapsed into silence.

"Look," I finally broke the tension between us. "I'll be careful. You'll see. Besides, you can't resist me."

She resisted, but then smiled. "How about that pizza?" she said, changing the subject again.

» » » » »

The next morning I was up by seven, early for me. I hadn't slept very well after leaving Willie's place. I had no idea that she felt the way she did. We had been playing a flirting game for some time, but I really never thought that I'd been making any headway. Not only was I wrong about that, it never occurred to me that if she did like me, she wouldn't want to date me because of what I did for a living. I thought only my parents hated my being a detective.

I pondered the previous evening while I went for a jog. Things had gone okay. We had decided on Chinese instead of pizza, and had a local restaurant deliver Moo-Shu chicken and garlic pork. We added an inexpensive white wine, and dined by candlelight on her back balcony while we watched the sun disappear behind the downtown high-rises. I told her a little bit about my latest case, she told me some of her hospital stories. But we never touched on what she shared earlier. It was like an emotional wall had been erected, and neither of us was sure how to break it down.

As I ran, my frustration built, and not just on a physical level. I enjoyed spending time with Willie, and as I inched ever closer to my mid-thirties, I was becoming more conscious of wanting to share my life with someone. And when the one woman who cranked my chain finally came along, my job was getting in the way.

I went five miles, and by the time I rounded the corner of my block, my legs were burning. I slowed to a walk, cooling down. Maybe

Willie would cool down a bit, too, and I could make her see what she was missing. What could be more appealing than a financially secure, recently-employed-as-a-detective male?

I took the stairs two at a time up to my condo, ate a quick breakfast, and showered. I threw on a pair of jeans and a white Izod shirt and drove to the office. I tackled a few mundane work things, like checking through my mail, mostly bills, returning phone calls to two potential clients, watering the two hanging vines in the front reception area, and responding to emails.

In every batch of emails that I received, I could count on one from my parents. My mother, retired in Florida with my father, loves the usefulness of email. She's quite the typist, having spent a number of summers working as a secretary in a huge law firm before she met my father, who took her from average Jane to wealthy Jill. Since those long-ago workdays as a transcriber, her skills are used to email friends and relatives. And I am one of the lucky few who receives at least a weekly update from her, long diatribes on her every moment since the last time she either wrote or called on the phone. I love my mother dearly, but I wish she could only type a few words per minute. Then maybe I wouldn't have to read about each card game with the Smiths and Joneses, their close retiree friends, or about my father's health issues, which always amount to nothing more than a slight case of gas or indigestion.

Just as sure as ice cream melts in the Florida sun, there was an email from Mom. I wrote a quick note back to her, lamenting with her about Dad's pending visit to the doctor for his yearly exam, assuring her that everything would be fine, telling her that my job was indeed going well, and that I was working on a new case. My parents had not been enthused when I launched my detective business. Dad thought it didn't qualify as real work unless you worked with a Fortune 500 company and earned a steady paycheck, and Mom worried constantly that I would get hurt. She and Willie would have to battle for the rights to that, I thought, as I typed her assurances that I was safe and sound.

Once that was done, I searched the Internet to see what I could find out about Ned Healy's death. One article gave me the facts of the discovery of Ned's body, and another two follow-up reports shed light on the investigation into his death.

Ned Healy's body had been found outside of Buena Vista, off County Road 162 where the Mount Princeton to Raspberry Gulch ride begins. A pair of riders first reported his abandoned car at the trail head. It had been parked overnight on the side of the road. Three days later, a different set of riders on the trail spotted Ned's bruised and torn body, along with his dented mountain bike, at the bottom of a thirty-foot ravine. He hadn't been wearing a helmet, and his shirt and shorts were not specifically designed for mountain biking. An autopsy performed on the body determined that Ned had trace amounts of Seconal, a barbiturate, in his bloodstream, and he had a blood-alcohol level more than twice the legal limit. The official cause of death was a broken neck caused by his fall. With the help of witnesses who remembered when the car appeared at the trail head, authorities believed that Ned was riding late in the evening while very intoxicated, and that he lost control of his bike and went over the ledge, falling to his death. Ned's death was ruled an accident.

I had never ridden that trail, but had heard of others who had. It wasn't a very difficult trail, overall, but there were a couple of more technical areas to traverse. A novice rider could get off and walk through those parts with no danger of personal injury. But anyone on a mountain trail could succumb to an accident – that was one of the risks in the sport. Ned's death may have been nothing more than an inexperienced rider trying to tackle too difficult a trail.

I found another article discussing potential risks of mountain biking, which referenced Ned, and obituary listings. That was all. Nothing suspicious. I sat back and stared at the poster from *The Big Sleep*. Bogie looked so tough in that poster, so sure of himself. He had it so easy, though – the plots already had an ending, and Bogie always won.

My phone rang, breaking me out of my reverie. It was Jack Healy.

"Reed, I'm glad you're there. Do you think you could meet me at Ned's house?" His voice sounded like a tuning fork, ringing with apprehension. Or fear.

"Sure," I said, glancing at the clock. "What's going on?"

"I stopped by Ned's house on my lunch hour, and it looks like the place has been broken into."

"I'll be right over."

I hung up the phone, grabbed my keys and rushed out the door. I had just found something suspicious.

# CHAPTER FIVE

I assumed Jack must take an early lunch because when I drove up to Ned's house in, it was barely after eleven and Jack was here instead of at work. I stepped out of my nice air-conditioned 4-runner and the summer heat hit me like a dry wave. As I walked up the drive past a blue Volvo, I took a good look at Ned's house – it had neglect written all over it. Due to water restrictions in the metro area, most of the neighborhood lawns could've used a little more water, but Ned's was like wheat bread, with just a few green patches that needed to be cut. It seemed even more rundown than the first time I was here. A few newspapers were strewn on the porch, and some flyers were stuck in the front screen door. The exterior desperately needed a coat of paint, a drainpipe was torn away from the house, the windows needed a washing, and dried-out rose bushes with wilted buds screamed for water. Jack opened the door as I approached.

"Come on in." He gathered up the newspapers and tossed them inside the door onto a growing stack. More neglect for Ned's house. "Thanks for coming," Jack said as I closed the door behind me.

"Sure." I stepped into the living room after Jack. A stale smell hit me, and the heat engulfed me like a stifling blanket as I glanced around. The house was so sparsely furnished I couldn't tell if anything was disturbed. "Have you called the police?"

He shook his head. "I wanted you to see things first."

"But what about prints, stuff like that?" I asked, even though I didn't believe any would be found.

"I don't think they're going to find anything," Jack echoed my thoughts. "A back window was jimmied open. Nothing seems to have been taken, but someone rifled through his records. The file cabinet door was left open, and I'm positive I closed it when we left the other night."

"You're sure nothing was taken?"

"I think so. I guess I didn't look that closely. I doubt if I'd notice a file or two missing anyway."

"Let's call the police and report this," I said. "No sense in messing up a potential crime scene."

Jack agreed and used his cell phone to report the break-in, then called his work to say he would be later than he first thought. When a police officer arrived, Jack explained that the house belonged to his deceased brother. The officer was not enthusiastic about finding a burglar, but he took a report, and asked if anything appeared to be missing. When Jack said he didn't believe so, the officer said Jack shouldn't keep his hopes up. With that, the officer left.

"Now that I can touch things without contaminating a crime scene," Jack said with light sarcasm, "let me open some windows." He threw back the blinds of the living room window, and in seconds a slight breeze blew in, just enough that the fresher air from outside rejuvenated the inside air.

"Where's the goldfish?" I asked, noticing the empty spot where the tank once sat.

"I took him home to my daughter. She'll take good care of him."

I nodded, secretly pleased that the little guy had a home. He and I'd had a connection.

"Let's take a better look at Ned's files, and make sure you don't notice anything missing," I said. "If someone wanted to see the files bad enough to break in, there might be something gone."

We headed down the narrow hall to the office. The tiny bedroom was just as stuffy as the rest of the house, so I took Jack's lead and opened the window first thing. It helped a little.

"Have you really checked all his real estate files?" I asked.

"I started to. I examined the first few carefully, then thumbed through the rest, but it's all just legalese to me."

I wasn't sure it would be any different for me. I grabbed the handle of the top cabinet drawer. "Aren't these files confidential?"

Jack shrugged his shoulders. "You're a detective. Can't you bend the rules?"

"Bend, yes. Break, no," I said. If I don't know what the rules are, is that breaking them? I thought. A philosopher in my own mind.

Jack stared at me.

"Oh hell." I yanked open the drawer and perused the files, all neatly gathered in manila folders. Ned had alphabetized the files, so "Anderson" was the first in line. With as much enthusiasm as I could muster, I took the folder and sat down at the desk. The file was an inch thick, filled with all kinds of paperwork, forms for inspections, notices, and every other kind of documentation possible for the purchase of a house. My whole life didn't have this much paperwork associated with it.

"Why don't I start at the end," Jack said, grabbing a folder from the back of the drawer. He sat down on the floor and rested the paperwork on his lap.

I rummaged in the desk drawers for a pad and paper, having left my standard, Hollywood detective-issued notepad at the office. I found a spiral notebook in the middle drawer with a bunch of pens, so now I was set.

"Did you talk to Samantha?" Jack asked after a few minutes.

"Uh- huh," I said. "I got exactly nothing from her."

"She was a bitch, right?" he said. "I'll bet she slammed the door on you."

"How did you guess?"

The corners of his mouth twitched up as he tried to hide a smile. "She did it to me when I showed up to tell her about Ned. His death didn't even faze her."

"No?" I looked up. "She wasn't sad at all?"

"No. She got mad at me, then ordered me to get off her property. Like I said, she hated Ned and she hates me."

I mulled that over, then turned back to the records I'd been reading. After ten minutes I was bored and having trouble focusing on the papers. I kept hearing a nearby dog bark with every passing car. A sprinkler started in a yard somewhere. I shifted in the chair. It squeaked loudly. I tried to concentrate. Five more minutes and the only thing written on the pad were some notes that Ned had written.

I glanced at them, at first thinking I was reading a description of a sculpture of some kind, but then I realized that the notes described of all things an Oscar statuette, the famous Hollywood Academy Award:

2-Karat bronze statue, gold-plated

13" tall

Weight: 6 ¾ lbs

Base made of marble

Statue stands on an 8-slotted movie reel


What the heck were those notes doing along with his real estate notes? "Did Ned like the Oscars?" I asked.

"I don't know," Jack said. "He liked seeing movies, so maybe."

"Huh," I tried to wrap my fingers around a sense of who Ned Healy was. All around his notes were doodles, numbers, an address, and, a bit oddly, I thought, a list of colors: blue, gray, white, yellow. Whenever he'd written that stuff he'd been as bored as I was right now. Or maybe he was playing some kind of trivia game.

"I don't have any idea what to look for," Jack broke the silence.

"I don't know. A pattern. Numbers that don't add up." I couldn't help feeling like I was wasting my time. A beer and a few games of pool sounded so much better.

We managed the task for just over an hour. At that point, I'd been through more than a dozen files, and I felt like I would see real estate data in my dreams.

"This is nuts," I said, pushing paperwork across the desk. "We'll never find anything this way."

Jack sighed. "You're probably right. But what do we do?"

I was tempted to say, "Maybe there's a secret compartment, and if we push the right book on the shelf, a door will magically appear. Inside we'll find what we're looking for." I resisted though, raking my hands through my hair in frustration. "If somebody did take a file, we wouldn't know it."

"What if they just wanted information?"

"We could spend all night looking at these files and not see what's missing, or incorrect," I said, my frustration palpable. "I've got a better idea." I turned to the computer and switched it on.

"As long as Ned didn't password protect anything, we can access the electronic files."

"How does that help us?"

"I have a friend who might be able to tell if any of the files don't look right." The computer sang a jingle at us, and the desktop appeared. I didn't notice anything that might be real-estate related, so I hit the start button. Under "Programs" I found what I was looking for. HousePro was in the list, the only one with a real estate reference in its name. I opened the program. A window opened with a list of documents. At the end were folders, labeled by year. Ned was more organized here than in his file cabinet.

"There!" Jack leaned over and pointed at the screen. I glanced at him, wondering if he always pointed out the obvious.

There were about twenty files. I opened one and saw that it was a standard contract, just like many of the ones we'd been reading. I still didn't see anything fishy, but Cal might.

Cal Whitmore was my best friend. He was also the Holmes to my Watson. Cal rarely left his home in the foothills west of Denver, preferring to work within the confines of his home office. He was the ultra computer geek, as well as an all-around genius. He'd know more about these files than I ever would.

"I wonder if Ned's Internet access is still working," I muttered.

"I haven't cut the phone or cable or anything," Jack said hopefully.

"He must have cable or DSL. Something." I didn't care what, as long as I could email the files to Cal.

I hit the icon for the Internet and sure enough, I found I was able to access the World Wide Web without any problems. In a couple of minutes, I had connected to my own email account.

"I'm glad he didn't password protect this," I said.

The safety freaks were death to detectives like me. Ah, the things that Bogie didn't have to deal with.

I pulled out my cell phone and hit a button, which automatically dialed Cal.

"Yeah," he said after two rings.

"You have time to help me with something?" I asked.

"What's up?" Cal didn't waste time with words.

I explained what I needed.

"Aren't those files confidential?"

"I don't know," I said, not wanting to discuss my rationale. "That's never stopped you before."

He chuckled. "I guess I deserved that one." The term hacker could've been invented for Cal, and I knew better than to ask what all he did on his computer. "Send the stuff over. You don't know if the files are on the up-and-up or not?"

"They probably are," I said. "I'm stabbing in the dark."

"Okay. I've got some work to finish this afternoon before I can get to it. Give me until the morning." I knew he'd spend all night if he had to. I didn't know how Cal managed to operate on so little sleep, let alone how he managed to figure out the things he did.

"Thanks," I said and hung up.

"Who was that?" Jack asked.

"A friend of mine. He's a modern-day Sherlock Holmes. He knows everything about everything."

"I wish I could retain stuff like that," Jack said.

    I nodded agreement while I set up the email and attached half of the files, and sent them off. No use taking the blame for Cal's lack of sleep by making him look at all the files. If he was successful, I could send the rest of the files over. "He'll take a look at them and see if anything looks fishy," I said to Jack.

    He leaned on the edge of the desk. "Think he'll find anything?"

    "You'd know better," I said.

    "Uh-huh." Burt Lancaster's Swede couldn't have said it better.

# CHAPTER SIX

Cal let me down. It was actually early the next afternoon before he called me at my office.

"I'm not sure what you wanted me to find," he said when I answered the phone.

"Nothing?" I asked. I honestly didn't think he would unearth anything, but I was holding onto a sliver of hope. I was surprised at my disappointment.

"Not nothing. But not much either." I could hear the tapping sound of Cal typing on the keyboard. I pictured him, sitting at one of his many monitors in a room cramped with computers and computer equipment, discarded takeout boxes and trash lying around, a film of dust on everything but the precious electronic equipment. And since Cal was practically a computer himself, he fit right in. "Most of the files you sent were standard real estate files. I didn't notice anything fishy with any of them."

"You said most."

"Right. There were two that struck me as a little weird. Not illegal, just odd."

"Odd how?"

"One of the buyers had an unusually short time to back out of the deal. Typically, you build into a contract a clause where you're able to back out, or cover yourself if you can't sell your home first. And if you really want the new house, you make sure there's plenty of time for you to sell off your old one first. Or you put in a contingency that says you have to sell your old home before you purchase the new one. One of the contracts doesn't seem to do that."

"But that's not illegal, right?" I asked.

"No, just unusual."

"Which one?"

"Wilson," he said.

"And the other unusual one?"

"Owens." I heard more tapping sounds. "On this one, everything looks fine, but there's a whole list of items the buyer wanted changed after the house inspection. You usually don't ask for too much, even in a buyer's market. If you do, the seller can say no to the changes, and the contract is dead. Then, you wait until someone else is willing to pay more, or wants fewer changes. There's more profit that way."

"So Ned's buyer asked for too much, and the seller didn't want to do that. Is that in the contract?"

"Yeah. There's a form voiding the contract because of the inspection. I'm emailing you both files now. On the Wilson contract, look at the time frame. It shows a period of only a couple of weeks for the sale. Pretty short, but again, not illegal."

"Why would someone do that?" I said, "other than to get out of the contract?"

"Exactly. You need anything else, let me know." Cal knew his role as my right-hand man, and that I'd probably be calling on him again.

I checked my email, and the two files that he sent were waiting to be opened. Once I saved them on my hard drive, I opened the first one, for Bert and Amy Wilson.

Bert and Amy – sounded like something out of *Sesame Street*, I thought with a chuckle.

If Jack had read this file before, he apparently didn't notice what Cal had. Not that I thought Jack would've, since he knew about as much about hokey real estate deals as a drunk knew about virgin drinks: they were out there, but you'd never seen them.

I went to the page that Cal had said looked fishy and read through the text. He was right. I thought back to when I bought my condo, and how much time I wanted to get everything done. If I'd had a place to sell first, I would've needed that done before I bought the condo, and that could've taken a while. The time frame on the Wilson contract seemed a bit short, but that didn't make it illegal. So why do that?

I found the name of the seller's real estate agent: Eric Townsend. I looked up the name and called him. I got voice mail that said to leave a message, or if I wanted I could try Eric on his cell phone. Lest he miss a potential customer, I thought. I jotted down the number and dialed it.

Two rings and he picked up. "This is Eric." I could hear static and road sounds in the background, indicating he was driving somewhere.

"Eric, this is Sam Spade," I said. One of Humphrey Bogart's most famous roles was also my favorite *nom de plume* when I didn't want to be me. "I was a friend of Ned Healy's. I don't know if you heard about him."

"Yes, that was unfortunate," Eric said, although his tone didn't match the sentiment. "I've worked with him on a deal or two."

"That's what I'm calling about," I said. "Trying to wrap up a few things with his estate, you know." Eric uh-huhed on the other end like he was commiserating with me. "I was looking at the Wilson file. Bert and Amy?"

"I know the one. That deal fell through." Eric spoke in a high, squeaky voice, like an angry mouse.

"I see that. I noticed that the time frame for them to sell their house was less than a month. Isn't that a bit short?"

The connection broke in and out, then I heard him say, "…can't say what happened."

"What's that?" I asked. "You don't know what happened?"

There was a long pause, filled with static hiss. "Who did you say you were?"

"I'm a friend of Ned's." He was being cautious now. I knew I was losing him, and not just because of a bad connection. "I'm just trying to close out the Wilson file. Ned had a note on it, wanting to make sure the Wilsons were okay with how things turned out."

"Oh, is that all?" The edge left his voice. "I really shouldn't be telling you this, but the Wilsons had changed their minds. They didn't want to sell their home after all, so they left the time frame short." Static cackled through the line.

"You were breaking up," I said. "You said the Wilsons didn't want to sell their house?"

"Right. They realized they'd made a mistake, that they didn't want to sell their house and move, but they already had a contract on it. That contract included a clause that made the sale contingent on their being able to close on a new house. So they put a contract on another house, but made sure that that contract would fall through by including a really short closing date. Once that happened, they could back out of the contract with the buyer of their house." What a trusting guy, to tell me so much. But, most people will say way more than they should just because they like to hear themselves talk.

"I see their predicament," I said. Sympathy can get you almost anything, too.

"I assure you that's not how things normally happen," Eric responded quickly. "But what could I do?" He began the job of CYA. "I didn't know what they were thinking until things started to unravel."

"I understand," I said.

"The Wilsons are happy, and so was the buyer of the home that the Wilsons originally wanted. I know their realtor, and she worked everything out."

"All's well that ends well."

"Exactly," he said.

I hung up, sat back, and stared up at Bogie on the wall. *The problem with the world is everyone is a few drinks behind,* he seemed to say.

I pretended to raise a glass to him. "I'm behind," I said. He silently concurred.

I looked up the name of the real estate agent listed on the Owens file, the second contract that Cal thought was unusual. That agent, Fred Gallegos, didn't answer, nor did he have voice mail or a cell phone number. I thought all real estate agents had about ten numbers to try, but I guess Fred valued his privacy more than the others.

I found the number for Garrett Owens in the file and dialed it. After four rings, a machine picked up. Duh, I thought, looking at the clock. It was just after one o'clock. Owens was probably still at work. I perused the file again and found a work number. This time I got a real person.

"Garrett here," a deep voice said.

Again I introduced myself as Sam Spade, and said I was a friend of Ned's.

"That bastard," Owens spat out. "You tell him for me that I hope he rots in hell."

I paused. "I can't do that," I finally said.

"Why?"

"Because he's dead." I gave him the Reader's Digest version of how Ned died, leaving out Jack's suspicions that Ned had been murdered.

"Oh," Owens said when I'd finished. "That is too bad, but I can't say that I'm sorry."

"Why is that?"

"Ned screwed me over. He was supposed to be my real estate agent," he emphasized the words harshly. "I'd never bought any property before, and he was supposed to be working for me. That's why you hire them, right? But not Ned. He helped me find this really sweet deal on a house, but then he messed it all up for me."

"How'd he do that?" I was curious now.

I heard a sigh that carried all Owens's disgust and disappointment with Ned. "Look, I'm only thirty, and it's harder than hell for someone my age to get ahead. I want to invest in some property while the prices are down. We found this great old house in Cherry Creek," he said, referring to an area of expensive homes just southeast of downtown Denver. "It was a bit of a fixer-upper. At one time it must've been a great home, and expensive, but compared to what they're building there now, or renovating, it needed some work. Anyway, it was perfect for me. I'm pretty handy, and I could see putting some time and money into it, and

I'd have a nice profit on my hands. Or I thought I might just sit on it for a while, and sell it to a developer."

"What happened?"

"That bastard Ned screwed things up for me, and the deal fell through."

"How'd he do that?"

"The place needed work, like I said. But after the inspection, Ned told me I should ask to have a bunch of the stuff fixed up as a part of the contract. He said there were things that I shouldn't have to worry about, things that every buyer asks to have fixed. And I listened to him. I had a whole list of things that I requested the seller fix, and if she didn't, I would back out of the contract. Hold on a second." I could tell Owens had covered up the phone, and I heard a muffled conversation in the background. "I'll get that to you," he told someone else, then "Sorry about that," to me.

"No problem," I said. "So you lost the house."

"Yeah," he said, regret replacing anger.

"But why are you mad at Ned? He could've been giving you what he thought was the best advice."

"Because he had a back-up buyer," Owens said, the bass voice getting louder and angrier again. "He had someone else lined up with an offer that was above the seller's asking price. That meant a bigger commission for Ned, but he had to get me out of the way first. That's why he told me to ask for all the repairs."

"Isn't that unethical?"

"Damn straight. I was so mad at the guy I never wanted to see him again."

"How'd you find out all that?"

"I contacted another agent, and she did some digging. I don't think she was supposed to tell me anything about the new contract, but I think she knew how angry I was. And I won't tell you who she was, so don't ask. Ned was pissed off that I knew anything, and he went to her about it. The whole thing turned into a real mess."

"You talked to Ned about all this?"

"Yeah, but he said his hands were tied. He denied making any suggestions to me at all, and said that it was all my doing to ask for the improvements, even though he was the one pushing me into asking for all the changes."

"Do you know who was buying the house after you?"

"Beats me," he said. "Why don't you ask Ned? Oh, uh," he stopped. "Sorry. I didn't mean that."

"It's okay. Was the seller's agent..." I flipped through the file, "Anthony Wolinski?"

"Yeah, that sounds right. Look, that's all I know. I washed my hands of the deal and Ned Healy. If I see him on the streets, I'll—." He paused again, realizing again that unless Ned had figured out a way to cross over from the other side, he would never be walking the earth again. Owens definitely had a case of foot-in-mouth disease. "Never mind."

I thanked him and hung up.

Ned Healy did not seem to be a very popular person, I thought as I sat at my desk, mulling over the conversation I'd had with Garrett Owens. Owens seemed to have the same kind of volcanic anger that Samantha Healy had toward her ex-husband. I wondered if Jack was aware of how others perceived his brother.

Did Ned screw over more clients in addition to Owens? I

wondered now if I'd stumbled upon a motive. Did Ned have back-up buyers on other homes so that he could make more in commission? Or was the house Garrett Owens lost the only one with a back-up buyer? And if that was the case, what did Ned hope to accomplish? Based off of his monetary records, he certainly didn't have the cash to invest in a house that needed renovation. Was Ned helping someone else, and benefiting in some way from that? I didn't know a lot about the houses in Cherry Creek, but I knew that real estate values in that area had been skyrocketing for a number of years. Someone could stand to make a lot of money on a house, or the lot, just like Garrett Owens had planned on doing. Was Ned in on a deal with someone?

Another thought pinged my brain. Would Garrett Owens kill out of anger? Let's face it, I knew nothing of the man, only that he had an incredibly deep voice, and he was incredibly angry with Ned.

I needed to investigate this further. I grabbed my car keys and headed out the door.

# CHAPTER SEVEN

210 Madison Avenue was a scant mile from the posh Cherry Creek Mall, with its high-end department stores, expensive boutiques, movie theater, and plenty of restaurants. The surrounding neighborhoods were filled with mid-20th-century homes that had become a beacon for the upper-middle class, although many of the smaller homes in the area were quickly being demolished and replaced with huge monstrosities that touted all the latest amenities but held none of the charm of the older homes they replaced.

The summer sun sat in a cloudless blue sky as I parked my 4-Runner a few car lengths down from the house that Garrett Owens had lost in the contract snafu. I grabbed the Owens file and walked along a cracked sidewalk to an appealing red brick bungalow with a long covered front porch. The separate garage was located behind the house and was accessed from the alley. The house would've been considered good-sized by the standards of its day but was now dwarfed by brand-new two-story homes on either side.

A lawnmower engine hummed far off, but Madison Avenue was empty of people. A real estate sign plastered with a "Sold" banner stood in the yard, and I jotted down the realtor's number. I climbed the three steps to the door and could see why Garrett Owens thought Ned had duped him.

On the outside, the house didn't look like a "fixer-upper". The trim had a new coat of light brown paint, the windows were double-pained, clean, and in good shape. The front door was solid, made of sturdy oak. However, Owens' contract had asked for new windows and had noted that the exterior of the house was "in need of new paint." I tried peeking through the slats in the window blinds, wishing I could see more of the inside. The green Astroturf on the porch seemed the worst thing on the exterior of the house, but the contract didn't include that in its list of requested repairs.

I walked around the side of the house, examining it as I went. The rest of the windows along the way did not appear damaged in any way, the gutters showed no rust or holes, and I didn't notice any structural damage of any kind, no visible cracks in the foundation or on the sides of the house. However, Owens had noted a concern about the structure, speculating about issues due to the new construction on either side of the house. If he wanted to renovate the house, the concern would be valid, but if he had been thinking of just reselling the house to a developer, I wouldn't have thought that structural soundness would be an issue. I made a mental note to call Garrett Owens and ask him that.

A six-foot wooden fence surrounded the back yard. I spied an unlatched gate, so I opened it and continued on around. The yard was large, plenty big enough to raze the house and build a newer, bigger one, if someone chose to do so. I sat down on a plastic lawn chair and reread the contract. The other requested repairs were to the inside of the house. Old pipes and hot water heater. Cracks in the bricks of a basement fireplace. Worn paint. Things that most people would never ask to have fixed prior to purchase. I wished again that I could get a peek inside to check those things out.

I stood up and tried the back door. Locked, of course. But it didn't hurt to try. Maybe if I tried a secret, magic word, it would open. "Allakazaam, ohiogazima, shazaam!" I chanted.

And the door opened. I froze in disbelief. My chant had actually *worked*? Then I saw the rear end and a pair of baggy jeans backing out the door.

"Shit!" The man's face turned the color of his bleached-blond hair, his brown eyes widened. The mover's box he was carrying nearly slipped from his hands. "Who the hell are you and what are you doing here?"

"I was just looking around," I said, trying not to stammer. "I heard that the house was for sale."

"It's sold. Or didn't you see the sign?" The man, somewhere in his late twenties or early thirties, seemed to have recovered, his surprise turning to impatience. He shifted the box, freeing one hand. "You really shouldn't be here."

"I saw the sign, but I was just looking around." I pointed at the door. "I really wish I could see the inside."

"I'm sorry, you can't," he said, pulling the door shut behind him. I had no doubt it was still locked.

"Are you a realtor?" I asked, trying for an Oscar as "the interested buyer".

He shook his head. "I was hired." I waited for him to explain, which he reluctantly did. "To inspect the foundation. I was just heading out."

"Oh, I see," I said, hoping I sounded exceedingly disappointed. "There isn't any way you'd let me go inside, take a quick look around?"

"No, there isn't." He pushed past me, forcing me to take a step back. "You need to leave now."

I pursed my lips, stalling for time. "Are you…" That's as far as I got before I rethought my tactics. He sighed and stared at me. "Okay," I finally said. "Thanks for your time."

He didn't respond, but watched until I left through the side gate. I heard the gate latch slide into place. I was tempted to dash back and spy on him through the cracks in the fence, but when I glanced over my shoulder, I could see his shadow on the other side, peering at me. So much for that idea.

I walked slowly back to my car, turned it on, and cranked the A/C. I waited to see if the guy would emerge and go to a car, but after five minutes and two songs by *The Police* I still hadn't seen him. He must've been parked somewhere in the alley, so he was long gone.

I contemplated going back to the house to see if I could find a way in when an old man in faded overalls emerged from a ranch-style house across the street. He stepped off his porch, knelt down, and started digging around rose bushes. Judging by the bags of compost and box of tools at his disposal, as well as his dawdling pace, he was going to be at it a while. Scratch searching for an illegal entry.

But I was curious. Were the problems Owens listed that bad? Either he was lying to me to cover up something, or Ned had found a first-class sucker to manipulate. But why would Ned risk possible ramifications from an irate client for a bit more in commission? It was time to look at the file for the back-up buyer that had bought the house.

# CHAPTER EIGHT

"I should make you a key," Jack Healy said as he unlocked the door to Ned's house. "That way you wouldn't have to wait until I get off work." He smiled broadly as he held the door open for me, and I swear he was Burt Lancaster. Spooky.

"Thanks." After leaving the house on 210 Madison, I had again arranged to meet Jack at Ned's house so I could have another go-round with the real estate files. The back-up buyer's file for 210 Madison, if I could find it, seemed to hold the key.

"Man, it gets hot in here," Jack said, loosening his tie and rolling up his sleeves. "I take it your coming back here means you found something."

"I don't know," I said, going straight to the file cabinet in Ned's office. The office didn't seem as stuffy as the last time, but Jack cranked open the sole window in the room, then went to the other rooms in the house, opening windows. I immediately felt a soothing cross-breeze.

I dove into the files, searching for the proverbial needle in the haystack. "What are you looking for?" Jack asked when he returned.

"There should be another file for 210 Madison," I said. "If Ned kept it, that is."

"Let me help." Jack knelt down, opened the bottom drawer and started examining files. It was a faster process than the last time we were here, since we now only needed to check the address lines for 210 Madison.

Just as I yanked open the second drawer, Jack stood up, banging his head on the underside of the drawer. He cursed, rubbing his head with the file folder he was holding. "Here it is: 210 Madison."

I took the folder and sat down at the desk.

"What's in it?" Jack asked, continuing to rub his head.

"Don't know," I mumbled, scanning the pages. I noticed the new selling price first. It was only ten thousand more than Garrett Owens' offer. That meant Ned would've only made a few hundred dollars more in commission. If that was his reason for sabotaging Owens' contract, it was negligible. However, given Ned's apparent financial situation, a few hundred might have seemed more than paltry. If he did this kind of thing a lot, the money would add up.

I pulled out my cell phone and called Cal. "You didn't find multiple contracts for the same house?" I asked, explaining what I'd discovered with 210 Madison Avenue.

"No, but you didn't send me all the files either."

"I'll send the rest that were on Ned's computer. He has more files here, too, so I'll still have to go through those."

"Oooh, more paperwork. Yuck."

I hung up and sent an email to Cal with the information. Then I turned to Jack. "I need to go through the files again and see if there are any with more than one contract for the same address. It might take some time."

"I'll help." He pulled open a drawer and grabbed a bunch of files. "You continue with that file, and I'll do these. I've got a good memory, so it shouldn't take that long to check them." Having something to do seemed to bolster Jack's mood.

I kept reading through paperwork on 210 Madison until I found the new buyer's name: Dominic Saunders. I flipped a few more pages until I found his contact information. He lived in an apartment in Northglenn. A home phone was listed, but no work or cell phone numbers.

"Here's the new buyer for 210 Madison," I said, picking up my cell phone again.

Jack glanced up at me from the floor where he was thumbing through stacks of file folders. "What's this guy going to tell you?"

"I don't know." I could tell that the mundane aspects of detective work did not appeal to Jack. If he knew how often I chased my own tail...but we won't get into that. Let's just say it's not all excitement and danger.

I dialed the number for Dominic Saunders. After one ring I heard a recorded message stating that the number had been disconnected. I hit the end button.

"What?"

"Disconnected," I said. "How was Ned supposed to contact this guy to complete the sale?"

"Is there another number?"

I checked the file thoroughly, but found no other address or phone number. "Wait a minute." I checked the dates on the file. "Closing was supposed to take place two weeks ago."

"But Ned was gone by then." Jack stood up and returned the folders to the file cabinet, taking out more and setting them on the floor.

"Who took over the real estate deals that Ned was working on?"

"There were only two pending deals that I was aware of," Jack said. "I contacted the clients and they were going to get new agents."

"But what about this Saunders file?"

Jack examined the papers more carefully before shrugging his shoulders. "It never came up."

I scratched my head. "That leaves a couple of possibilities. Either Dominic Saunders went with another real estate agent and he didn't bother to tell you, or his contract was voided, just like Garrett Owens."

"You're not going to blame Ned again." Jack's voice rose defensively.

"No, but if Saunders is out of the picture, and there's now a third buyer, I need to find out who it is. Saunders should be able to clear some of this up."

Jack was quickly scanning files while we talked. "What are you going to do?"

"I guess I'll be going to Northglenn." I got up and returned to the file cabinet. "What's left here?"

"Just those last few." Jack motioned to the top drawer. "I better finish, since I've looked through all the others." I handed him the last few files and he perused them. "It's easy once you know where to find the address information." After a minute, he closed the last folder and handed the stack of files to me. "I didn't see any duplicate addresses."

"So," I said as I shut the cabinet drawers, "that eliminates any here. I'll see what Cal finds, but it's appears that 210 Madison was the only property that had a back-up buyer." I rested my arms against the top of the cabinet, mulling over my conversation with Garrett Owens. "If there were more duplicate contracts, I could see Ned scamming people to make extra commission. But since there aren't more duplicates, I'm not seeing how Ned would benefit by sabotaging the Owens contract."

"Maybe you're missing something."

I stared at Jack. "Obviously."

He threw me a sour look, crossed to the window, and closed it before leaving the room. "Maybe this Saunders guy can fill you in on what's going on. But I have to tell you, what you're describing doesn't sound like Ned. He was always an honest guy. I can't see him trying to wheel and deal for more commission, or for anything else."

I snatched up the files for 210 Madison and followed him into the master bedroom. "Maybe so, but this real estate stuff is the only thing I can find that doesn't seem to add up. And I wouldn't get my hopes up, if I were you. It's probably nothing."

"I'm not," Jack said as he cranked the handle on the window and shut it. "If you come up with nothing, I can live with that. As long as my concerns are answered. Excuse me." Jack went into the bathroom and shut the door.

I didn't know if I could ever answer his concerns, I thought. I didn't know if anyone could. I stood and stared at the framed *The Maltese Falcon* poster while I waited for Jack. The poster was a very nice reproduction, the version where Bogie has a gun pointed toward you and he looks so suave. What made this particular poster even more interesting was that his haircut was different than it was in the movie – by the time the poster was produced, Bogie was sporting his shorter haircut from *High Sierra*. The poster was in great shape. It looked so similar to *The Big Sleep* poster I had, so *film noir*, so classic. So my taste. I tried not to drool over it.

I gestured at the poster when Jack returned. "You don't have any idea where Ned got this?"

"No. Some poster store or eBay, I would imagine." He took it off the wall with both hands and studied it. "Just a cheap poster, if you ask me. You want it?" He held it out to me.

"Sure," I said, downplaying my enthusiasm. Not just everyone appreciated *film noir* as I did. I tucked the poster under my arm, grabbed the folders for 210 Madison Avenue and followed Jack out of the room.

"Keep me posted," was the last thing he said to me before leaving the house. I doubt he caught the pun in his words.

» » » » »

Forty minutes later I was at the Mountain View Apartments in Northglenn. Located in an out-of-the-way neighborhood dominated by huge pine and aspen trees, the complex of five buildings had an appealing feel of seclusion. Dominic Saunders' address listed in the file was on the second floor of Building 3, Apartment 2D. I rapped on the door twice and studied the parking lot as I waited. The parking space for 2D was empty.

I knocked again, then glanced at my watch. It was now almost eight o'clock, and the sun was just dipping below the horizon, golden rays filtering through the tree branches to the west of the building.

I looked all around and saw no one, so I cupped my hands and peered into the window near the door. The blinds were drawn, but I thought I could see in just enough to tell the living room was empty of furniture. I tried the door, but it was locked. I knocked once more, but had lost hope of anyone being home. It appeared likely that Dominic Saunders no longer lived there.

I spent a few minutes trying to find a rental office. I finally located it in a separate building across a small courtyard, but it had been closed since five o'clock.

I strolled back to Building 3 and tried the neighbor in 2C. No one was home. The whole complex was as quiet as a cemetery. It took me another minute to find the bank of mailboxes near the office. Most had nameplates on them, but 2D's was blank. Imagine that.

I turned around to go back to my car just as a Jeep 4X4 pulled up. A young man in faded jeans and Oxford shirt got out, digging keys from his pocket.

"You wouldn't happen to know if the guy in 2D moved?" I asked him.

He barely noticed me as he opened his mailbox. "No, I don't. I'm in building 4."

"Do you know anyone in building 3?" As I asked the question, I stared at the guy. I knew I'd never met him before, but something about him. I couldn't place it.

"Yeah, but she works evenings. You might try the rental office tomorrow."

I stared at him. "Do I know you?"

"Don't think so." He retrieved his mail and hopped back in the Jeep, tires screeching as he drove off.

I walked slowly back to my car, picturing his face, hearing his voice. Then it hit me.

I raced back to the 4-Rrunner, unlocked it, and grabbed the files for 210 Madison. I found it in the file for Garrett Owens. It was right there and I hadn't even noticed it. Owens lived at the Mountain View Apartments, Building 4, Apartment 3A.

I snatched up the files, locked the car, and jogged over to Building 4. I took the steps two at a time up to the third floor. 3A was at the tops of the stairs. A stereo was playing inside. Jimi Hendrix sang about being a voodoo child as I pounded on the door. A few seconds later, the volume dropped and then the door opened.

Garrett Owens had changed from jeans and Oxford shirt into a pair of black cycling shorts and a light blue jersey. He was pulling on riding gloves and I could see a road bicycle leaning against the wall behind him.

"Oh, it's you again." He reached for a blue and white cycling helmet on a coffee table. "I told you I didn't know whoever you were looking for."

How could I have missed that deep voice?

"You're Garrett Owens," I said.

"Yeah?" He raised his eyebrows in surprise. "How do you know me?"

"I'm, uh," I had to reach back to recall what name I'd used. "Sam Spade. I talked to you earlier about the house on 210 Madison."

He had the helmet on, tugging on the dangling straps. "The guy on the phone. I told you everything I know about Ned Healy." He was pulling so hard on the straps, I thought he might break them. "How did you find me?"

I held up the file. "It wasn't that hard." I didn't want to tell him that it was his voice and not my skill at detection that led me to his door.

"That's my real estate file? Is that what you're telling me?" He crossed his arms and glared at me. "Isn't that private information? How did you get that?"

Oops. "I'm a friend of Ned's. I'm trying to wrap up his business affairs, which would include his real estate records." I held up the folders as proof, of what I wasn't sure, but it felt good to do it. "After I talked to you, I read through the new contract on the house."

"And that buyer lives here?" Garrett appeared genuinely stunned.

Or he was pulling off an incredible acting job. "You're kidding me."

"No." I leaned against the doorjamb. Jimi finished singing, replaced by the Red Hot Chili Peppers. "You want me to believe that you both put a bid on that house, but that you didn't know each other? Yet you both live in the same apartment complex?"

"Yeah, because that's the truth." He tried to stare me down. "What else could it be?" he finally said.

I didn't say anything.

"You don't think losing the deal was my fault, do you? Why would I do that?" He took a step forward, pointing a finger at me. "I don't know who you are, mister, but that contract fell through because Ned Healy told me a pack of lies. Yeah, I was dumb enough to believe him, but being a dumb ass doesn't mean I did anything wrong. And just who the hell do you think you are coming here and bugging me?"

"Where were you on the night of June 6th?" I asked, sounding just like a bad television cop show. I couldn't believe I'd just said that.

"What?" He choked back a snort. "I haven't a clue. Riding, probably."

I backed up. "You and the other buyer both living here is just a coincidence?"

"Yeah, it is. Now leave me alone." He slammed the door shut, and this time, I didn't try to stop it with my foot. Fool me once...you know the rest.

# CHAPTER NINE

I was up early the next morning, my sleep restless and filled with dreams about missing keys, Jack Healy as The Swede in *The Killers,* waiting in a dim apartment waiting for his murderers, and Humphrey Bogart helping me find the Maltese falcon that was buried in Ned Healy's backyard. Maybe it was the pepperoni and onion pizza I ate with the Goofball Brothers when I returned home the previous night.

I showered and dressed casually in Dockers and a polo shirt, ate a quick breakfast of orange juice and a bagel, and drove to the office, carting along the Bogart poster that Jack had given me. I had decided on the ride home from the Mountain View Apartments that I would hang it in my office alongside my other *film noir* poster.

First thing on my list was to call the seller's agent for 210 Madison Avenue. I leaned the Bogart poster up against the wall, under the framed poster of *The Big Sleep.* I contemplated where to hang it as I dialed the number. After two rings, he answered.

"I'm Franklin Hardy," I began, elated that I had actually reached a person and not voice mail. "I'm interested in 210 Madison Avenue, and was hoping I could see the property."

"210 Madison?" I heard papers rustling in the background. "That's under contract right now."

"Yes, I'm aware of that, but I'd like to see the house anyway."

"I'm sorry, Mr., er, what was your name?"

"Hardy. Franklin Hardy." Unless he was a reader of the Hardy Boy mystery series, I didn't think the name of the duo's detective father would ring a bell.

"I hate to tell you this, Mr. Hardy, but the house is unavailable." He didn't sound like he hated telling me that; he sounded gleeful. "I've got a solid contract on it now, and we're just waiting for the closing date, so there's really no point in seeing the place."

"I'd love to look around the house anyway. The designs of those old homes are fantastic."

"I really can't allow that." I detected a note of irritation in his voice.

"Who's the buyer? Maybe I could talk to him or her about that?"

"I can't divulge that information, Mr. Hardy. Is there anything else I can do? Show you another home? I'm listing some other nice properties in that area."

"Let me give that some thought, and I'll get back to you." I disconnected before he could get his sales pitch into gear.

I perused the files for 210 Madison Avenue and found the number for the owner, Edna Mills. An answering machine responded on the fourth ring, but I hung up before the techno-voice finished speaking. I noticed her current address was in Evergreen, a mountain community west of Denver. I mused on some ideas and formulated a plan.

I picked up the phone again and dialed. "I'll be there at ten," I said without fanfare, "and we're going for a bike ride."

"No," Cal whined before I'd finished. "It'll take us almost two hours to get there, and I've got too much to do."

"You'll have it done before I can say Dick Tracy, genius. You said you'd do this, so no more excuses."

"All right." I heard a creative string of obscenities as I hung up the phone.

>> >> >> >> >>

"Do you know how tempting it is to run you right off the trail?" Cal huffed at me.

"You have to catch me first." I pumped hard, my legs burning as I rode up a steep incline. On either side of the trail, aspen and evergreen trees towered over us, branches intertwined like locked fingers. At the base of the trees, parched bushes and other scrub brush created thick, dry foliage, a firefighter's worst nightmare. Fifteen feet behind me, Cal was pedaling furiously and losing ground fast.

"I should never have let you talk me into this." Cal had agreed that he would put aside his disdain for the outside world and go cycling with me at least once a week throughout the summer. This was our second trip and I had my doubts that we'd make it a third. I didn't know how much of his grumbling I could take. But when I glanced back a time or two, I almost saw a smile crease his sweaty face. Underneath all his grumbling, I think he was beginning to enjoy himself.

For a while the only sound came from our bikes and our lungs. The air smelled fresh and clean, and a slight breeze carried the scent of pine. I pushed the pace until I found the spot I was searching for.

"Here it is," I said, coming to a stop at a rock outcropping. We were on Mount Princeton trail, at the same spot where Ned Healy had fallen to his death. The trail traversed partially buried boulders that made a wavy, washboard pattern before joining the dirt path on the other side. The exposed rock surface was about three feet from side to side, with a sharp drop-off on one side, and a cluster of trees on the other. Someone had tied a red ribbon head-high on a tall pine tree. I wondered if it was a reminder of Ned's death or another accident.

"Whoa," Cal said, screeching to a halt behind me. "You're crazy if you think I'm going over that."

"It's not too bad, if you stay close to the trees," I said.

Cal craned his neck to look out over the ravine. He couldn't have gotten much of a look from his vantage point by the trees. "Is this where Ned died?"

"Yes." I got off the bike, leaned it against an aspen tree, and walked along the trail, my eyes roving around. I stared down at where Ned had fallen. If someone rode too close to the edge, a slip of the tires or a bad turn of the wheel could send them over. I shuddered.

"What do you do if you don't want to ride over this?" Cal asked.

"You get off and walk." With exaggerated movements, I showed him how easily I was walking over the rocks. The guy was a computer genius, but take him out of his element...

Cal nodded, but he stayed put, balancing on the bike with one foot on the ground.

"If two people were riding this, it wouldn't take much for one person to shove another person over," I observed. "Stick out your foot and nudge them. It could easily be made to look like an accident."

"If it's that easy, why do they let people come through here?"

"They don't. Remember that turn we took back there? This is an old part of the trail that isn't generally used anymore. But in the woods like this, you can't do much to stop people."

Cal nodded again, but still didn't move.

I walked back to my bike. "Ready to go?"

"I'm not going over that."

He gripped the handlebars, his knuckles turning white. The look on his face told me I'd have better luck trying to move the mountain than to move him across the trail.

"All right. Let's head back to the car." I turned my bike around and mounted.

"Now you're talking." Cal whipped his bike around, but before he could get going, I was already ahead of him. I kept a steady pace as we pedaled back over the trail.

"Just a little farther," I hollered after a bit.

We rode in silence for a few more minutes, and I let him catch up. "I need another favor."

"Being your cycling partner isn't enough?" Cal wheezed, standing up on his bike as we bounced over a rocky part of the trail. "Dragging me to a place like that?"

"This is fun." I leaned forward, working hard.

"Yeah, tell that to my legs." Cal huffed for a moment. "Don't you even want to know about the other files you sent, or was finding that place on the trail your only mission?"

"I was going to ask what you found out, but since you can't wait..."

"It's really not that exciting. I didn't notice duplicate addresses in any of the files." He sucked in a few breaths. "The one on 210 Madison is the only one that Ned had two contracts for."

I eased back as we headed down a slope, braking carefully so my tires didn't slide. "I didn't find any on the hard copies either. That shoots my theory that Ned was scamming buyers for extra commission."

"What else did you need?"

"I want everything you can find on Garrett Owens and Dominic Saunders. And see if you can find where Dominic moved to." Although the Internet was full of sites claiming to do background checks on people, using Cal was almost like having access to an FBI database: if there was something to find on someone, Cal would unearth it. I didn't ask how, but it was easier than me trying to do it. And Cal didn't charge me anything for his services.

"And see what information you can get me on 210 Madison Avenue. Old real estate records, liens, anything unusual about the house," I said.

"That shouldn't take very long." Cal may not be athletic, but on the computer he was Michael Jordan, John Elway, and Wayne Gretsky all rolled in one. I could spend days searching for the information that he would have a slam-dunk-hat-trick before the first quarter was up. "What's so important about those guys?" Cal's breathing had slowed enough that he could almost carry on a conversation without wheezing.

I explained my visit to the Mountain View Apartments, and bumping into Garrett Owens. "I still don't get why Ned would try to lose the deal for Garrett, but it sure seems like more than coincidence that Ned had a back-up buyer who lived in the same complex as Garrett."

"Maybe Garrett talked to Dominic about it."

"Only two more miles back to the car," I yelled over my shoulder, pushing for a burst of speed.

Cal kept pace with me as we rode down the trail and back to my 4-Runner.

"You owe me," he said, gulping for air as he skidded to a stop.

"Your heart thanks you, and cedes any payments I might owe."

Cal arched his eyebrows. "Does your mother know what you're

doing to me?"

"Oh, that's cold," I said.

Cal chuckled as he helped me load the bikes onto the rack on the back of the car.

"Why would Garrett talk to someone in his apartment complex about buying a house?" I mused, thinking about what Cal had said.

Cal held up a hand as he caught his breath, then wiped the sweat off his face and neck as he talked. "Maybe the two were chatting while they got their mail or something, and Garrett says too much about this great house he's buying. Dominic sees dollar signs and then decides to put his own bid on the house."

"Could be," I said, pulling my car keys from my jersey pocket. "But that doesn't explain Ned's involvement with both of them. And Garrett is still pretty angry about the whole thing."

"Angry enough to kill Ned?"

"I don't know."

"Okay, you figure it out, Sherlock." Cal chuckled as we piled into the car. "How are your parents?"

Cal and I had been friends since we were little kids and played on the same soccer team, and he was like family. Cal was quite familiar with my mother's fear that I wouldn't meet a nice lady, settle down, marry, and have a few kids. Producing grandchildren was her sole goal in life. That and getting me out of the detection business. Since I'd been shot in the rear, on my first case, nothing could've pleased my mother more than if I'd give up my profession and find a more respectable and less dangerous job.

» » » » »

I showered, cleaned up and changed clothes at Cal's house, then left him to his research while I drove down Highway 285 to Highway 73. I took a left at the shopping center, a well-known landmark for people traveling from Denver to the Evergreen and Conifer areas. I followed the road for a couple of miles until I came to a section of houses on the left, each built on at least an acre or two of land.

I slowed down and watched for numbers on mailboxes until I found the address for Edna Mills. She lived in a quaint log style home up a long driveway, with a wide front deck and an awesome view of the mountains.

I drove around a circular drive and was just getting out when a light blue Lexus drove past me and pulled into the garage. I heard a door open, then slam shut as I approached.

"Ms. Mills?" I asked as a plump woman in her sixties emerged from the garage with a couple of bags of groceries in her arms. She was smartly dressed, with gray curly hair, dangling gold earrings, and pink lipstick that matched her dress.

"Yes, I'm Edna. How can I help you?"

I introduced myself as Philip Marlowe, not wanting to overuse Sam Spade. "I'm interested in the house on 210 Madison Avenue. It's such a good price."

"Oh, that's already been sold. Didn't your realtor tell you that?" She had a low voice, just a bit gravelly, but her smile was soft and pleasant. "We listed it low so that it would be sure to sell, you see. We had such trouble the last time we put it on the market."

"When was that?"

"A couple of years ago. My father owned it. But he had such trouble because it's an older home. No one wanted a fixer-upper, you see, so he finally gave up the idea. This time around, my husband said we should just list it so low no one could resist buying it. And we sold it." She beamed at me.

"Yes, I heard that, but I was hoping to get a look inside. I'm interested in the architecture of those old homes."

"There's nothing unusual about that home. My parents bought the house when they moved from New York, and Dad lived there until he passed away. That's why we're selling it, you see." She shifted the groceries in her arms. "What did you say your name was?"

"Philip. Can I help you with that?"

"No, let me just set them down." She placed the bags on the front deck. "*Why* are you interested in that house?"

"I'm studying architecture. So many of the homes in that area are being torn down and I wanted to take some pictures of the remaining ones," I said, "before they get demolished."

"That's nice." Edna pursed her lips. "I'm afraid there's not much to see in that old house. Dad wasn't able to keep it up in his last few years."

"I'm sorry about your father. It's tough."

"Oh, thank you, but it was months ago, and we knew it was coming. Cancer, you see, so we had a lot of time to prepare." Edna seemed to let her guard down. "And it took months to get all his records together, and to take care of the will. Then my husband Peter threw out his back, so it just took ages before we were finally able to clear the house out and prepare to put it on the market. And then with all the contracts falling through, it's a wonder we ever got it sold."

"How many contracts have fallen through?"

"Oh, just two," she said with a rusty laugh. "We're on the third now, so let's hope it's the charm."

"Why didn't the other buyers work out?" She was making this so easy for me. I wondered if she'd be so trusting if I resembled Al Capone.

"The first one asked for so many changes. Peter and I didn't feel we needed to spend that much on the place. We were selling it at a great price, after all. We would've made a few repairs, you see, but he wanted so many, and most of the things were not just minor changes. I know the house could've used some spit and polish, but we didn't feel like that was something we should have to do before we put it on the market. But structural concerns, walls sagging, the furnace?" She let out a heavy sigh. "The second buyer's financing fell through, you see."

"The financing fell through?"

She nodded sadly. "Yes, and so soon after his realtor passed away. The realtor committed suicide and then his buyer had to find a new realtor, and then the buyer couldn't get a loan. It all happened so fast."

"What was the new realtor's name?"

"Oh, I'm not sure." Edna put a finger to her lips, tapping as she thought. "I can't remember, and I don't believe I have it written down anywhere." She shrugged. "Now this third buyer seems right, a nice couple with a baby on the way. He works at a bank downtown and she's a teacher. They're so nice, you see, cute as can be."

I interrupted before she could tell me more about the couple. "Do you think they would mind if I saw the home? You could let me in."

"Oh, I don't think I could ask them that."

"But they seem like such a nice couple." Like I really knew anything about them, but Edna seemed sure.

She pursed her lips. "I don't think I should ask. It wouldn't be proper, you see. Why don't you wait until they move in, and then you could drop by and ask them yourself?"

I did see. I gave her my number in case she remembered the name of the second buyer's new realtor, thanked her, and left. Maybe it was because she sounded so much like my own grandmother, but I just couldn't make myself push her more.

## CHAPTER TEN

On my way down from Evergreen, I mulled over the case. Three buyers had been interested in the Madison house: Garrett Owens, Dominic Saunders, and now a new couple, who were actually buying the house. A house that Edna Mills said needed some work, but not huge structural changes that Owens had asked for. I needed to see the inside of the house, and since all my attempts at getting in had so far been rebuffed, I thought it might be time to do something different.

I turned onto 1st Street and was soon driving down Madison Avenue, slowing as I passed 210. Dusk had set in, creating long shadows from the tall trees growing on either side of the street. I didn't see the neighbor across from 210, but his rose bushes and rhododendrons bloomed with gusto. I continued to the end of the block and parked around the corner, behind a white van.

I got out of the 4-Runner, snatched the realty file off the passenger seat and locked the car. I sauntered down the alley, scanning the backsides of the houses until I reached 210 Madison. The one story home was easy to peg among all the newer, bigger homes. I glanced around and saw no one, so I tried the alley-access gate. Since it wasn't latched, I darted through and shut the gate behind me. I crossed the lawn to the back door of the house. Locked. I expected as much.

I stood there for a moment, thinking. I wondered if there was a lock-box on the front door. I slipped around the side of the house, through a gate and into the front. I quickly strode to the porch. Bingo. A little box dangled from the doorknob.

If I could somehow get the code, I'd be in. But how would I get the code? The new realtor had most likely changed the combination, but what if he or she hadn't? If Ned had it written down somewhere, I could at least try the combination and see if it worked. I quickly checked the file, but didn't see anything that looked like a combination. I made a mental note to go back to Ned's other files and check for any lock-box information that he might have written down. I made another mental note to ask Jack for a key to Ned's house so I wouldn't have to bother him again.

I hurried around to the back again and examined the lock and the deadbolt on the back door. Just in case I couldn't find the lock box code. I had very little experience in breaking-and-entering – okay, none – so I didn't have a clue as to how easy or difficult it would be to pick the lock. Mental note number three: ask Cal what he knows about this. Or more accurately, see how I could bribe him into coming down to Denver to help me, if it came to that. I was sure he knew how to pick a lock – he knew everything. Except how to leave his house on a normal basis.

To the left of the door was a large square window facing the back lawn. Dusk had given way to darkness, and I couldn't see into the house. I planted my face against the window, cupping my hands to the glass to shut out the glare. A face stared right back at me.

I yelped in surprise and fell against the side of the house, my heart pounding in my chest.

The back door opened. "What the hell are you doing here?"

I stared at the face of the same inspector I ran into the other day.

"Didn't I tell you the house sold?" the inspector snarled.

I nodded mutely.

"Well?"

I found my voice. "I was in the neighborhood. Thought I'd get another look."

"I told you before, you can't. Have you ever heard of trespassing?"

"Hey." I held up a hand. "There's no need to threaten me. I'm going."

But if I could find a key, I'd be back.

"Wait, I'll walk you to your car."

"No need for that." I started to back off the porch, but he disappeared in the house, emerging a moment later with a small box and a long tube, one that might hold pictures, posters, or anything else you might want to roll up instead of fold. Like architectural plans.

"Are those plans for the house?" I pointed at the tube.

"Huh?" He fumbled with the door before pulling it shut behind him. "Yeah, for the inspection."

"Can I see them? That would give me an idea of the layout of the house."

"No." With that abrupt response, he jerked his head at me, indicating I should get moving. We walked through the back gate and out into the moonlit alley.

"Where are you parked?" he grunted at me.

"Over there." I gestured down the alley, hoping that would be enough, but he followed me all the way back to my car and watched as I got in and drove off. As I turned the corner I could see him in the glow of a streetlight, still staring at my car.

"Curses. Foiled again," I said aloud as I turned on the CD player. The Smiths, one of my favorite 80's bands, sang tongue-in-cheek about being miserable as I drove around the block. I kept my eyes open for the inspector, but I didn't see him. He was long gone. That left me miserable with Morrissey and The Smiths.

It was almost nine o'clock, but I swung by the office. I wanted to check the Wilson file, the one where the sellers ended up not selling. In my experience, it seems that people tended to use the same passwords or locker combination numbers more than once – it cut down on having to memorize too many. If I could find a combination to the lock-box, which I hoped might be written in that file, I could go back to 210 Madison right now, when I knew the inspector wasn't there. Not ideal to go in the dark, but it would work.

I pulled out my after-hours pass key and slid it over the magnetic detector, waited until the light turned green, and yanked the door open. I passed the elevators and took the stairs up to the second floor. It was deathly quiet and dark as I walked down the hall and into my office. The windows near the elevator let in a haze of moonlight, making the ficus plants in the hallway appear to jump out at me. As I unlocked my office door, I caught a shadow out of the corner of my eyes. "Bogie wasn't scared of the dark," I whispered to myself. Ignoring the shivers that ran down my back, I flipped on the lights and grabbed the mail on my way into the inner office.

I tossed the envelopes on the desk and opened the Wilson file. I checked every piece of paper in it, front and back, and all the sticky notes tacked to various pages, searching for the combination to the lock box. Nothing. I wondered again if I might find something at Ned's house, somewhere in the real estate records where he might have jotted down a combination. The thought of reading through his files a third time nearly gave me a headache. And would it be worth it? If a new realtor had changed the combination, I couldn't get in anyway.

I glanced at my watch. 9:15. I was fresh out of ideas, so it was time to call it a night. I locked up and drove home.

» » » » »

As I started to climb the steps up to my condo, I noticed Willie drive up and park across the street. I hopped off the stairs and sauntered over.

"Just getting home?" she asked me as I waited for her to get out of the car.

"Working hard," I said. "Wanna help?" I smiled, trying to gauge her mood.

"With what?" Curiosity was a good sign.

"You could spy on a house for me," I said as we strolled up her front porch steps. I'd been pondering how to get into 210 Madison, but I'd also need to know when people were coming and going. I could do it myself, but surveillance was the most boring part of detective work.

"No way," Willie said as she unlocked her front door. "That's the most boring part of detective work."

I had to give her that. "What if we did it together?" I leaned on the doorjamb and cocked an eyebrow at her.

"You are incorrigible," she said, pulling me into the living room. "Besides, I have a job."

"It was just a thought."

"Come on in. I could use a beer." She headed toward the kitchen. "Want one too?"

Hmm. Go home alone, or spend some time with Willie and a beer?

I stepped into the room and closed the door.

## CHAPTER ELEVEN

I awoke the next morning with birds chirping, angels singing and news of world peace. Okay, nothing that big, but I'd been at Willie's until the wee hours of the morning. I was in my bed alone, but by the time I'd left Willie's house, after three beers and a lot of light chatter, I knew I was making some headway with her. My Wheaties had never tasted so good.

Once I was showered, I dressed in a pair of blue jeans and a white shirt and headed down to my neighbors. It was close to nine, so Ace was already at work, but Deuce might still be at home. Since he worked as an assistant manager at a local video store, he kept odd hours.

I knocked on the door twice and was about to give up when Deuce answered.

"Dude," he said with an ear-to-ear grin. "How ya doin'?" He stood there in jockey shorts and a faded gray T-shirt, and he rubbed sleep out of his eyes as he talked.

"Sorry to bother you so early," I said.

"It's okay," he said with a lion-sized yawn. "I had to close the store last night, but I should be getting up. You want a cup of coffee?"

I declined, but followed him through his cluttered living room and into the kitchen, where he poured himself a cup of sludge that had probably been on the warmer since his brother left hours earlier.

"I have a favor to ask," I said, taking a seat at a '50's-style chrome table. "Are you free today?"

"It's my day off, so shoot." Deuce sat down and poured a healthy dose of sugar into his cup.

"Would you be interested in watching a house for me?"

Deuce looked up from his methodical stirring. "Watch a house? You mean like on TV or something?" He seemed bewildered.

I shook my head. "No. Spy on a real house, watch to see who comes and goes. You keep saying you want to help me. This would be a big favor." And it would keep me from getting bored.

Deuce took a slurp of his java-like drink, then drew his hand across his lips to catch the excess liquid. "Sounds kinda boring."

I wasn't going to be able to *give* this part of the job away. "Okay," I let out a sigh. "I know it's not that exciting, but you said you wanted to know what I do, and this is part of it. I can pay you – "

"No, no," Deuce interrupted. "You don't have to pay me. That's what friends are for, right? I'll do it, at least when I'm not working. And I'll get Ace to help when he gets home. Besides," he shrugged his shoulders. "Maybe it'll be fun. Like Sylvester Stallone in *Cobra*, or Clint Eastwood doing Dirty Harry. Do I get to carry a gun?" The more he chattered about it, the more excited he became. Deuce as a detective – like Colombo and Forrest Gump rolled into one. Scary.

"Sorry, no go on the gun," I said. He looked deflated. "But maybe down the road I could have you follow someone." His expression brightened. "Here's what I need you to do." I grabbed a pad and pen off the counter and wrote down directions to 210 Madison Avenue. "I want you to keep tabs on who comes and goes. It's going to be tricky because you'll have to try to watch the alley as well as the front, but you might be able to hear someone going inside even if you don't see them. Get a description of who it is and what time. Got it?"

Deuce nodded seriously. "Yep. I can be there all day." He lowered his voice. "Except if I have to go to the bathroom or get lunch."

"That's fine," I said conspiratorially. I had no great vision that I would get a totally accurate idea of what all happened at the house, but the Goofball Brothers might see enough to let me know if and when people went in and out of the house. If they could help for a day or two, I might be able to establish a pattern of activity, and then I could make my own move on the house.

"Do you have a cell phone?" He nodded.

"What's the number and I'll call it?" I asked as I pulled out my phone. "That way we have each other's numbers."

Deuced rattled off the number and I dialed it. I heard his phone chirp in the other room.

"But how will I know it's your number?" Deuce asked.

"It'll be on the phone," I said. "Under 'missed calls'."

"But," Deuce said slowly. "What if someone else calls me?"

I sighed. "Here's my number." I jotted down my cell phone number. "If you have any questions, or need anything, you call me. Okay?"

"Got it." He grabbed the piece of paper and stared at it. "I'll memorize it, so in case anyone captures me, they won't find anything that would point back to you."

I managed to keep a straight face, barely. "You don't need to worry about that. When can you go over there?"

"Now." Deuce leaped to his feet and snatched a set of car keys off a hook by the refrigerator.

I pointed to the boxers. "You might want to get dressed first."

He turned red. "Oh yeah."

"Good. I'll call later on to see how you're doing."

Deuce saluted and dashed off.

» » » » »

I left the not-so-efficient-but-available Deuce to his task, and drove to the office. Once I prepared a more palatable cup of java than what Deuce had offered earlier, I called Cal.

"Yeah?"

That Cal, all charm.

Once we'd dispensed with pleasantries, which consisted of him complaining about how sore his legs and butt were from our ride yesterday, I asked, "Did you find anything on Owens or Sanders?"

"Let me see." I heard the usual clacking on the computer keyboard. "First of all, I didn't find much on Dominic Saunders. He's twenty-eight years old, went to high school in California, and attended UCLA for a semester before dropping out."

"How did you get all that? I really wanted a check on a possible criminal record."

"I'm getting to that," Cal chuckled. "Saunders has worked at a variety of trade jobs – construction, plumbing, electrician, both in California and here. He moved here five years ago, by the way. He has no criminal record, a few speeding tickets, last one two years ago, but that's it. I found an address prior to the one at Mountain View Apartments, but nothing since then. My guess is he moved out of the Mountain View Apartments recently because I tried tapping into phone, cable TV, and electronic records, but I didn't find any new listing for him. Either his new phone and electric billing information hasn't kicked in yet, or he's staying with friends or relatives somewhere. Or he might've moved out of state – I only checked Colorado records. I didn't take the time to search his financial records, but I could." I knew what Cal wasn't saying – that kind of research could mean some serious hacking – more than he'd already done.

"No, that's okay. If I need it, I'll let you know." I rarely asked him to go to that level because it was both difficult and dangerous for him. I once asked him to check financial records for me, and the FBI eventually found that out – but that's another story.

"Garrett Owens, on the other hand…" he began.

"What?"

"He has a more colorful past. Owens is thirty years old – "

"I knew that," I interrupted, remembering my phone conversation with Owens.

"You want me to finish or what?" he laughed.

"Sorry."

"He grew up around here, graduated from the CU in Boulder with a computer science degree, and has worked a few different jobs in the computer industry. I actually found his picture on his company's website. Do you want me to email a copy of it to you?"

"No, I've met him, remember?"

"Oh yeah. Anyway, Owens has been jailed twice – once for disturbing the peace and once for a domestic disturbance. He's been cited twice for playing his stereo too loud, and has had numerous speeding tickets over the years."

"Do you know the details of the two arrests?"

"He was arrested for disturbing the peace after he was thrown out of a Boulder bar. Apparently he started a fight with some other guys. He was twenty-one, so it was probably a stupid thing that happens when you're in college." I mumbled agreement. Cal and I attended Harvard together, and we'd pulled more than our share of dumb stunts. Only we never got caught. "The domestic disturbance occurred two years ago. He and his girlfriend, who was living with him at the time, got into an argument. The neighbors called the police because they heard the two yelling, and with Colorado domestic violence laws that require one person in the dispute to be removed, Owens was taken to jail. He was put on probation for a year, had to attend court-ordered anger management classes, and pay court costs, and fines. He hasn't been in trouble since then. At least nothing that's documented."

"So Owens has a problem with his anger," I said. "Interesting."

"Uh-huh. He's lived at the Mountain View Apartments for three years, and before that he jumped around some. He pays his bills on time and has good credit. He shouldn't have any problems buying a house."

"Would he resort to revenge because of what Ned did to him?" I processed out loud.

"It's a possibility," Cal said.

"What did you find out about 210 Madison Avenue?"

I heard him typing again. "That house was built in 1942, along with most of the other original houses in that neighborhood. It's had four owners: David Meyers was there for four years, then it was sold to Horace Armstrong. He owned it for five years before selling to Eric and Alfreda Wainwright. They were there for sixteen years, then sold it to R. F. Gray. He's owned it since 1967."

"And now his daughter inherited it and is selling it."

"Yep."

"Doesn't sound like anything out of the ordinary," I said. "Did you find any records to indicate that the property is a bad buy, or that the area has soil problems or other issues that would cause structural damage?"

"Nothing. The way real estate values are in that area, it looks to me like it would be a great investment, especially since it's listed a bit below market value. Owens got screwed out of a good deal. He could've made thousands just in land value alone. Why is it listed so low?"

"Mrs. Mills said her father tried to sell it a couple of years ago, but no one wanted a fixer-upper. So this time around, they wanted it to sell fast with no hassles."

"I would think it would sell fast, at the price they're asking."

I had to agree. "Did you find anything on the latest buyer?"

"No. That stuff isn't official record until the closing, so there's not much I can get my hands on."

I hung up disappointed. I really wanted to get inside that house and see why Owens thought there were so many problems that he jeopardized his contract and lost the house. And if Ned really was the impetus for Owens losing the house, what did Ned gain? I couldn't figure that piece out, but I had a clearer picture of Owens. He had a track record of anger problems. Would he resort to murder because he was mad at Ned? It seemed more and more likely.

I still didn't have any way of contacting Dominic Saunders, I thought, while staring at the Bogart posters. If I could talk to Saunders, he might shed some light on all this. Or was there anything special about the house at all? Maybe it had nothing to do with Ned's death.

"Aw hell," I said to Bogie.

I decided to give my brain a break, so I focused on another important matter – where to hang my new Bogart poster. I picked up the poster of *The Maltese Falcon* and held it up next to *The Big Sleep* poster. Darned if they didn't look good together. Both had an aged quality to them, and Bogie looked spectacular, the quintessential detective. But the more I admired the posters, the more I didn't like the frame on *The Maltese Falcon*. It was made out of light wood, ash or pine, and it didn't look right next to *The Big Sleep* poster, which was in a black metal frame.

I set *The Maltese Falcon* poster down, rummaged around in my desk for a screwdriver, and went to work on the frame. In a matter of minutes, I had carefully extracted the poster from the frame. As I laid the poster on the floor, I noticed its pristine condition, and yet it still had the faded quality of old paper. I knelt down and scrutinized it some more. And I smelled the paper. Yes, I know that sounds funny, but something was nagging me. I stopped what I was doing and gingerly put the poster back in the frame.

I rummaged around in my desk drawer until I found a familiar business card. My hands shook as I dialed the number. If my hunch was correct, I needed help.

## CHAPTER TWELVE

Leaving traffic sounds and threatening black clouds outside and entering the imaginary world of movies, I stepped into Classic Hollywood Memorabilia. The shop was located in a long, narrow space stuck between two larger antique stores on south Broadway in the heart of Denver's "Antique Row", a section known for its multitude of stores and specialty shops that dealt exclusively in antiques.

As my eyes adjusted to the controlled lighting in the store, I saw a diminutive man at the back stand up and adjust his tie and pinstripe suit. He ran a hand over his white hair and tugged at the ponytail that touched his coat collar before he recognized me. Then a smile spread across his wrinkled face.

"'Allo, Reed. How are you?" Henri Benoit limped around the counter and shook my hand vigorously. "You have the poster, yes?"

Henri, a World War II veteran who injured his leg in the Battle of France in the spring of 1940, was a transplant straight from Paris. He had been a well-known and respected antiques dealer in France, but had also become an expert in Hollywood memorabilia, moving to the U.S. years ago to further that interest. Henri loved anything related to the movies, but had a special appreciation for the Golden Age of Hollywood, the 1930's and '40's. An avid collector himself, Henri turned his love of

classic movies into a thriving business, buying and selling vintage
posters, placards, props, autographs, and anything else related to the
cinema. He was also a noted appraiser, and his expertise was highly
valued in the collector's arena. His keen eye missed nothing, and for this
he charged high fees, which weeded out both the novice collectors and
the swindlers. "Would you like some tea?" he asked, finally letting go of
my hand.

"No, thanks," I said. "Here's the poster I told you about."

When I purchased my Bogart poster, Henri had appraised it to
make sure it was authentic. I knew I could count on him to check my
suspicions of *The Maltese Falcon* poster that Jack Healy had given to
me. After my tentative look at the poster this morning at the office, I had
called Henri, but he wasn't available until after lunch. I came to the shop
at two, barely containing my collector's excitement.

"Ah, what have we here?" Even though Henri had been in the
states for years, he still spoke with a stereotypical French accent, and
with a penchant to end all sentences with a question. He gingerly took
the poster from me and went behind the counter to the back of the store,
where he used a dime-sized side room as a work area. "Where did you
get this?" he called back to me as he laid the poster on a wooden table.

My eyes had been wandering around the small store, gazing
enviously at all the wonderful memorabilia for sale. There were posters
from a variety of old movies, autographed 8x10's of dozens of famous
Hollywood actors from Bing Crosby and John Wayne to Brad Pitt and
Tom Cruise, props, and clothing worn by actors. It was like walking into
a Planet Hollywood restaurant that specialized in the golden age of
movies, only all the memorabilia was for sale. I leaned on the counter
and could see him studying the poster. "A friend gave that to me."

"Come, come." He beckoned me to join him. "Let's get a closer look, eh?" He donned a set of bifocals and set to work on the frame, treating the poster like priceless artwork from a museum. "Ah, another Bogie movie. I'll bet you're drooling over it now, eh?" I laughed. Henri knew how fond I was of Bogart movies. He finished removing the poster and set the frame aside. We stared down at the piece of paper, appreciating it.

"Let's do a couple of simple tests," Henri said. He bent down and sniffed at the paper, then had me do the same. "What do you smell?"

"It's musty," I said. "That's one of the things that got me wondering about its age." Recent posters have a new smell to them, but old books, papers, and documents sometimes have a different smell, a stale, old smell like walking into an unfinished cellar. Smelling the paper wasn't a foolproof method of authentication, but it's a start.

Just then a bell above the store entrance jingled, indicating a customer. "Excuse me a moment," Henri said. He paused to straighten his tie before leaving the room.

I glanced over my shoulder and got a brief glimpse of the man who had come in, but I didn't want to be nosy about Henri's customers, so I occupied myself by calling Deuce.

"Hello?" he answered in a hushed voice.

"It's me," I said, talking in a low voice so I wouldn't disturb Henri. "How are you doing?"

"Fine," he whispered.

"Why are you whispering?" I whispered back.

"I don't want anyone to hear us."

"Who's there?"

"No one."

"Oh." I said, resuming a more normal voice level. "I'm sure you don't have to worry about that. Have you seen anybody going in the house?"

"Yes," Deuce hissed. "I saw a man go in the back door at 12:40. I wrote it down because you said to do that. He had a small cardboard box with him. He was inside for fifteen minutes, and he came back out with the same box."

"What'd he look like? Was he an inspector?"

"How should I know? He was just a guy."

If you don't ask a Goofball Brother for specifics, you won't get specifics from him. I should have known. "What else?"

"That's all. Except – " He stopped abruptly.

"I, uh… A neighbor saw me, Reed. An old man across the street. He asked me what I was doing hanging around."

"What'd you tell him?"

"That I was waiting for my realtor to let me in." I was impressed with his smooth thinking, and I told him so. "I saw the 'for sale' sign out front," Deuce said, with a touch of pride. "That's how I thought of it. I went around to the back of the house after that."

"Good job."

"You should talk to the old man, though."

"Why?"

"He says the house is haunted. He was giving me the creeps, talking about lights being on and stuff."

"Really?"

"Yeah. I don't want to be here at night, okay? In the daytime's fine, but not after dark."

"No problem," I said. I could hear Henri wrapping up in the other room. "I've got to go. Can you watch the house until six and then meet me at B 52's?" I knew that both Ace and Deuce should be home from work by then. "And see if you can get Ace to take over for you and watch the house when you leave."

"All right. I'll see you tonight."

While Henri worked out some details for appraisals, I put away my cell phone and looked closer at *The Maltese Falcon* poster. The quality of the paper seemed similar to my other poster. Almost all new posters use a heavier paper, but old ones were advertisements, not meant to have any long-term purposes, so they were printed on cheap paper.

Henri finished with his customer and came back into the room, and I told him what I had been thinking. "Yes," he said, tipping his head thoughtfully. "I noticed the same thing. Let's check one more thing." He scrutinized the entire poster, his eyes running along the edges and back and forth across the paper.

"Hmm," he mused. "The paper looks intact, no evidence that the edges have been tampered with." If a poster was a reprint, the name of a reprinting company might be printed on the edges. People often trimmed such things off the edges of a poster in order to make it pass for an original advertisement. He concentrated on the center, where Humphrey Bogart looked stern and Mary Astor looked stunning.

"Ah, yes," he finally said. "See?"

I looked where his finger was pointing, at a letter "B" in one corner of the poster. "Studios often included release information for a film, and also marked advertising posters with letters to indicate that it was part of a series of posters. The "B" would indicate that it was the second in a series of prints for the movie. I don't see an "R" anywhere on the paper, which would tell me that this was a re-released poster."

I felt my palms getting sweaty. "Are you telling me that this is an original advertising poster from 1941?" It couldn't be. Ned Healy didn't have any money to buy such a thing. Or had he bought it long ago, and Samantha and Jack didn't know he had it?

Henri pulled his glasses off. "Maybe. It could be a very good replica. I need to examine it much more closely before I can say for certain."

"Okay," I said. I stared at the poster again. Maybe I was getting excited for nothing. That had to be it. "There's no hurry. Let me know when you find out if it's a reproduction or not."

"Yes, I think I can fit it in. Business has been very good lately. This other gentleman that just came in, I've been working with him on some wonderful memorabilia. His collection is truly amazing, some very valuable pieces, but he is parting with some of it." He gestured at the poster. "But for you, I can make some time. I'll call you in a few days, maybe a week?"

"That'll be fine," I said.

"While you're here, you want a nice picture of Bacall?" he asked me with a sly smile. "She's very sexy, yes?" He took every opportunity to tease me about my adoration of Lauren Bacall.

"No, Henri," I said with a laugh. "Not today." A beeping interrupted us. My cell phone.

Jack Healy was on the other end. "I need to talk to you," he said before I could finish saying "hello." He sounded angry.

"What's going on?"

"It's Samantha," he said, spitting out the words. "I should have known it was her. She's as greedy as he ever was. If ever there was evil incarnate – "

"Jack," I said, discreetly turning away from Henri. "What about Samantha?"

"That bitch," he almost screamed. "She's getting a half-million dollar life insurance payoff."

# CHAPTER THIRTEEN

Jack Healy worked in one of the many lackluster-designed office buildings in the Inverness Business Park, south of downtown.

As I turned off County Line Road, a typical Colorado afternoon thunderstorm began, dumping gallons of rain in seconds and slowing traffic. I drove east until I came to Jack's building, a silver three-story sprawling complex on the south side of the road. I pulled into visitor parking, got out and dashed through the downpour. By the time I skidded through the sliding glass doors to the reception area, my shirt stuck to me like another layer of skin. As I made an attempt to appear more presentable, I asked for Jack Healy. A petite brunette who sat behind a large, curved desk pointed to the elevators, saying I should get off on the third floor, where a receptionist would escort me to Jack's office.

"Thanks for coming," Jack said when I entered his spacious office. He stood up and leaned over a long oak desk to shake my hand. The receptionist pulled the door shut behind me without saying a word. "Have a seat."

I plopped into a soft chair with green cushions and stared back at Jack. Behind him was a huge set of bookcases filled with large black binders and a few knick knacks. Jack looked diminutive sitting amongst the furniture.

"How did you hear about the life insurance policy?" I asked. Jack had been so upset when he called that I thought I'd better go talk to him in person before he decided to go confront Samantha himself.

"Right, the beginning," Jack said, heaving a deep sigh. He ran his hands over his face, then got up and began pacing in front of a wall-to-wall window that had an expansive view of the Front Range, now obscured by the torrential rainstorm.

"I came back from lunch and there was a message to call my lawyer." Jack waved his hands around as he talked, emphasizing his words. "No big deal, right? I get calls from him all the time. But this time, when I call him he says that he just got news of a life insurance policy that Ned took out after he and Samantha were first married, and did I know about it."

"Did you?"

Jack glared at me. "No. This was news to me, and that's what I told John, my lawyer. So I said give me the details. It's a $500,000 policy with Samantha Healy as the beneficiary if Ned died by accident or natural causes, but the policy is null and void if he commits suicide."

"That's standard."

"I know. But what I want to know is why Samantha's name was still on the policy. They've been divorced for over a year, so why would Ned still have her as the beneficiary?"

"He probably didn't get around to changing the name on the policy."

Jack crossed his arms and leaned on the window ledge. "That's what John said. He also said he looked at the policy and it's correct. There's nothing wrong with it, so Samantha will get the payoff. The insurance company contacted him about the specifics of paying her.

That's when he called me." His eyes narrowed as he looked at me. "Don't you get it?"

I gazed at him thoughtfully. "I know where you're going with this. If Samantha knew about the policy, she could've killed Ned, made it look like an accident, and then she gets the money. One of the oldest stories in the book." I thought of *Double Indemnity* and other movies and novels with an insurance scam in the plot. Bogie would've loved this.

Jack's head nodded in agreement. "Yes! It fits."

"Don't get ahead of yourself, Jack. Ned's death was ruled an accident, and at this point Samantha is innocent."

"But it makes sense. Ned once said that Samantha never seemed to have enough money, so the insurance would get her that. And she refuses to get a real job. Did she tell you about her acting career?"

"Uh-huh. Missed an opportunity to work with Spielberg," I said. Jack snorted his disgust.

"Now she'll have plenty of money." Jack's anger fizzled out and he stared at his shoes. "At Ned's expense."

I sat in silence for a moment before saying, "I'll go talk to Samantha. But she may not have done anything to Ned. She's not guilty of anything yet," I reiterated.

Jack looked up at me. "Yet."

》 》 》 》 》

I fought Friday afternoon rush-hour traffic and rain as I headed west on C-470 to Samantha's home, but by the time I pulled into her driveway, the thunderstorm had moved further east, replaced by bright sunshine and a hazy rainbow arching over Denver.

The air conditioner in the car had nearly dried my clothes, but I took a moment to comb my hair before I went to the front door. It was almost five o'clock. Since Samantha didn't have a regular job, I was counting on her being home.

I rang the bell and waited. The air smelled crisp and clean, with a pleasant touch of moisture. I hummed one chorus of the *Jeopardy!* song before I heard footsteps approach. My last encounter with Samantha was still fresh in my mind, so I prepared to put my shoulder in the doorway.

"Oh, it's you," was all Samantha said when she opened the door and saw me. No slamming it shut, no cursing, just "It's you." Probably the worst reaction a man could get from a pretty woman.

She wore a skin-tight scarlet dress that was pulled down over her shoulders, and black heels that added six inches to her height. The dress was cut mid-thigh, exposing her long legs. She wore a generous amount of makeup, making her brown eyes bigger and her rosy lips more sensual, and her aura seemed less angry than the first time I met her. She was, in a word, hot.

"I need to ask you a few more questions," I said, getting right to the point. I didn't know how long her good mood would last.

"Okay," Samantha said as she put on a gold necklace. "But you have to make it quick. I'm expecting company."

"A boyfriend?"

She placed a hand on the doorknob. "If you want to ask about my personal life, you're wasting your time."

I raised a supplicating hand. "Just curious. What I really want is information about Ned's life insurance policy."

"So you've heard."

"Jack called me."

"What about it?"

"Did you know about the policy?"

"Sure. I felt it was important that our future was protected, in case something happened to Ned."

"Your future was protected, not his."

"If you say so." Her lips turned down in a pout.

"Why did Ned leave you as the beneficiary of the policy after you divorced?"

She met my gaze and held it. "I don't know. Perhaps you should ask Ned."

I was not amused. "Since we both know that's impossible," I said evenly, "I'm trying to ask those close to him why he would do that."

"I wasn't close to Ned. That's why I divorced him."

"And since he died, accidentally, you stand to get a tidy sum of money." She didn't say a word. "It would seem that he still felt close to you, so he left your name on the policy, or he just forgot to make a change." More silence. "I'd guess the latter."

"That's all you're doing – guessing." She spoke with a cool assurance.

My eye twitched in anger, so I counted silently to five. "Where were you when Ned died?"

"It's come to this? You think I killed Ned? Somehow I would've expected more from you," she said with a disappointed wag of her head. "I haven't seen him in almost a year, so how could I have killed him?" I waited. She drew in a long breath. "I was at my acting class until almost eleven. Not that it's any business of yours, but after class I came back here with a friend of mine. He was with me all night. I told the police that already."

"What acting class?"

"Higher-level method acting." It sounded like some kind of new age class to me.

"What school?"

"Denver Alternative College." I'd never heard of it.

"And the name of your friend?"

Her eyes became slits. "That's none of your business."

"Maybe your friend helped you."

"With what?"

"Killing Ned. You get Ned drunk, stoned on pills, then take him up into the mountains and run him off the side of a cliff. Neat and tidy. You have an alibi, and now you get the insurance money. Although you would have to split it with your friend. But that's the breaks, I guess."

Samantha stared at me, but said nothing. Just then a forest-green Lexus pulled into the driveway next to my car. A tall, sturdy man with reddish-blond hair got out and strolled over.

"Hello, Sam," he said to her, throwing me a tentative smile. He had the weary look of someone who had just come from work, with bags under his eyes and a tired expression on his face. He wore a gray three-piece business suit tailored to show off his sleek physique and bulky arms, and a silk tie loosened at the collar.

"Why don't you ask Alan yourself," she said to me.

"Ask me what?" His eyes darted from her to me and back to her again, lingering on her dress.

"Nothing, honey." She opened the door and Alan stepped cautiously past me and into the house. Once inside, he pecked Samantha on the cheek, then gave me a cursory glance, noting the silence between us. "Are you ready to go?" he finally asked her as he went on down the hall, obviously familiar with the house.

"Just a second," she called to him. She leaned towards me,

whispering. "Alan and I killed Ned for the insurance money – right. You should write screenplays. That's a perfect plot out of some B-grade mystery movie."

Or the classic *Double Indemnity*, I wisely chose not to say.

She stepped even closer, pulling the door partway closed. "This is the last time I'm going to say this. I don't know why Ned kept my name on the policy, but he did, and I'm not going to turn down half a million dollars. Not for you, and certainly not for that brother of Ned's. For the second time, I have been more than patient with you and your silly questions. If you bother me again, I'm going to get the police involved."

"If you change your mind, and there's something you want to tell me," I said, pointing to my business card, which I noticed was still lying on the half-table behind her, "you know how to reach me."

She whirled around, and in one swift motion, she plucked the card off the table and ripped it in half. "Leave me alone," she said, letting the torn pieces drop to the floor like snowflakes. By the force with which she slammed the door, I knew I succeeded in making her mad.

I stood on the porch a moment. So her apparent boyfriend's name was Alan. She let that one slip out. Alan who? And did my theory have even a hint of reality to it? Did Samantha know that Ned hadn't changed the name on the policy, and did she kill Ned, or have Alan help her kill Ned? She was right about one thing, I thought as I sauntered back to my car. It did sound like the plot from a B-grade movie.

## CHAPTER FOURTEEN

I stopped to grab a fast-food burger, and by the time I finished and drove from Samantha's to B 52's in downtown Denver, it was close to seven. I was well past the time that I'd asked Deuce to meet me, but I knew that the pool tables would keep him from missing me. It was Friday, but I was lucky enough to find a parking space in a lot kitty-corner from B 52's, and I walked the half block down, past happy-hour people enjoying the start of the weekend.

Inside B 52's the sound of '80's music, U2 singing about Martin Luther King Jr., blared from hidden speakers. The hostess at the door recognized me and directed me to the back where Deuce was in the middle of a game of pool.

"Hey Reed," Deuce said after he sunk the 9-ball in a corner pocket. He lined up his next shot but missed.

"I got you a beer." Deuce handed me a Fat Tire with condensation dripping down the side. "Ace is watching the house right now. He said he wasn't scared of any ghosts, but that he didn't want to stay past ten because he's got to get up early for work. He said to call him and he'll give you a report."

"That's great," I said, taking a sip of the beer.

"And he says you owe him a game of pool because he's missing out."

I smiled. "I can do that, too."

"Bob's meeting us here."

"Oh yeah?" Bob was the older brother to the Goofballs. I hadn't even known of his existence until he moved from the East Coast back to Denver a year ago. He had apparently taken the best of the Smith gene pool in the first round, leaving his two younger brothers to sort through the leftovers. Bob was an EMT and operated with a full deck – more than could be said of his siblings. But Bob had felt a first-born's concern to keep an eye out for his brothers, which prompted his cross-country move.

"We're trying to teach Bob how to play pool," Deuce said. The Goofball Brothers may not have gotten much from the gene pool, but they definitely had ownership of billiards talent. I'd seen Bob play a time or two, and he was horrendous.

"I win," Deuce said as he sunk the 8 ball in a side pocket. "How about a game?"

I picked up a cue, waited for Deuce to rack the balls, and then I broke them with a loud crack. It felt good, like letting the business of the day shoot across the green tabletop. As we played, I chewed on the events of the day: Cal's research on Garrett Owens and Dominic Saunders, my visit to Henri's shop, Jack learning about the insurance policy, and my conversation with Samantha. I couldn't shake a feeling like I'd missed something.

I wasn't concentrating, so Deuce beat me easily, and I suckered for another game. Deuce emerged the victor and had just challenged me to yet another game when his pupil arrived.

Bob Smith was a carbon copy of his brothers – or, since he was the oldest, I suppose the brothers were copies of him. Tall and slim, with soft gray eyes, Bob had an engaging smile and a gentle demeanor.

"Bob," Deuce said, clapping his brother on the back. He chattered excitedly, telling Bob about how he had helped me out.

"Trey," I said, shaking Bob's hand. He always smiled when I called him by the nickname I'd given him when I first met him and mistook him for a third and youngest Goofball Brother.

"Spying on a house," Bob said to Deuce as he returned my handshake. "Nothing dangerous?" he asked me, although there was a gleam in his eyes. He knew I would never do anything to harm the brothers, and that involving them in an investigation gave them a sense of importance.

"No," I said, explaining that I was curious about who was coming and going from a house that was for sale.

"That sounds more fun than pool," Bob said. Deuce grimaced, horrified.

"No way," Deuce said. To the Goofball Brothers, mocking pool and billiards was like blaspheming to a churchgoer. Deuce grabbed a cue stick and gave it to Bob. "You have no idea what you're missing out on. This is way better than detective work."

Bob grinned at me. "What's this latest case about?" he asked while listening to Deuce explain the finer points of handling the cue stick.

I explained what I had so far, which wasn't much. "So I've got an angry ex-client who thinks Ned cheated him, and an angry ex-wife who gets to cash in on a life insurance policy," I concluded.

"My bet's on the insurance money," Bob said. He rested the cue lightly on one hand, and attempted to aim at the cue ball. "So why is Ace still watching that house?" He pushed the cue forward and watched it glance off the ball. It rolled harmlessly past the remaining balls on the table. Deuce snickered.

"Try this," I said, adjusting the way Bob was holding the stick. "I don't know that there's anything going on at the house. I was curious about all the activity, but it might mean nothing. The ex-wife could be perfectly innocent, too. For all I know, Ned's death was an accident, just like the police deduced."

Bob hit the cue ball and it inched its way to a solid ball, barely nudging it. "Let me watch you guys." Bob stepped back and let his brothers play. "So where do you go from here?" he asked me.

I shrugged. "Research what I can on insurance policies," I said. "And check on Samantha's alibi."

"It's like one of your old Bogart movies," Deuce said. "Always chasing after the wrong thing."

"Yeah," I said glumly. Just like a movie, but with a critical piece of the plot missing.

I was perched on a bar stool, watching the brothers play when my cell phone buzzed.

"Reed, it's Henri." I had a hard time hearing the Frenchman because of the din of rock music in the background.

"Henri, hold on a minute." I ran outside and stood under the porch eave near the front entrance.

"I haven't been able to look at the poster in great detail," Henri said, "but I did some research on the availability of that particular print, as well as some pricing for an original, eh? I have quite a bit of research here, many notes on old posters. I thought you might like to see it all, so I left a message at the office, but I did not hear from you. I hate to bother you on your cell phone…"

"I haven't been back to the office since I left your store." I put a finger in my other ear to drown out the noise of people laughing and drinking out on the patio.

"My wife and I are going for a bite to eat, and I will be near your office. I could drop the notes off, eh? You could look and see what a find you might have."

A sense of exhilaration surged through me. His excited tone meant that Henri thought I might have an original advertising poster.

"That would be great," I said. I glanced at my watch – 7:30. "The front doors of my office building should be open until nine. Would that give you enough time? You could slip the notes under the door."

"Yes, that will do. I will finish with this other collector's memorabilia this week, and I will devote my full attention to your poster, eh?"

"Wonderful," I said.

I hung up, sauntered back into the bar and shared the news with Deuce and Bob. But even as we toasted my possible good fortune, I wondered why Ned Healy had the poster in the first place. Add it to the other answers that Ned had taken to his grave.

After chatting with the brothers for another hour, I left for the office to get Henri's notes. I was dying to know more about the poster and how much it might be worth.

» » » » »

The headlights of the 4-Runner cut through the darkness as I pulled into the lot on the south side of my building, illuminating numerous parking spaces. My office was close to the restaurants and bars that littered the surrounding streets, including the 16th Street Mall, a pedestrian mall in central downtown. Parking spaces in the evenings were usually at a premium. But this was a private lot, so I pulled into a slot near a BMW and a Lexus, the only other cars parked there. I got out and locked the door and, after shoving a few bills into the self-pay kiosk, I walked around to the front of the building, passing a lone couple who were headed in the direction of the mall.

I took my after-hours pass key out before I noticed that the green light on the magnetic display pad was on. That meant the doors were unlocked. I stepped up to the glass doors. The right one wasn't quite shut.

Weird.

The latch was stuck in place. I couldn't free the lock mechanism, even after poking at it with my keys, so I left it alone. I'd alert the building supervisor about the problem tomorrow.

Most of the lights in the building were off, but at intervals a few fluorescent lights down the hallways glowed eerily, barely illuminating the gloomy lobby. I usually took the stairs to my office, but as I walked in the gray light toward the stairwell door, I had a sudden sensation that I was in some horror movie. The killer is behind the door, and even though you're screaming at the actor not to open the door, he does it anyway, only to meet a gory death from a crazed madman wielding an ax. I hesitated, then turned and strode across the lobby to the elevators.

"Stupid," I mumbled to myself as I punched the button for the third floor. I got on the empty car, and the big silver doors slid closed. With a soft humming sound, the elevator ascended.

I stepped out and walked slowly down the hall to my office, resisting the urge to glance surreptitiously over my shoulder. Paranoid about nothing, I thought. Isn't the human psyche amazing? All it takes is a little darkness and silence to set off waves of fear.

I chuckled as I unlocked the door and let myself into the outer room, stooping to pick up a couple of pieces of paper that were stapled together. I checked up and down the hall, but saw no one. Still, I bolted the door behind me. Just in case the bogeyman was out there.

I crossed to the inner room and flipped on the desk lamp. I sat down and perused the notes Henri had slid under the door.

The first page was a color printout of my poster, along with some website addresses that Henri recommended I go to for more information about vintage Hollywood posters. On the next page, Henri estimated that, if it were an original, *The Maltese Falcon* poster would be worth more than $12,000, depending on the market. Since collectibles were the rage right now, Henri thought his price was on the conservative side. The particular print I had was one of the rarer prints for the movie, with very few good copies available. Henri ended his notes with a paragraph stating that he would still need to do some sophisticated testing before he could determine if the poster was real and not a forgery.

My curiosity was piqued, so I turned on the computer, peering out the window while I waited for it to boot up. People walking down below looked like phantoms, featureless figures moving along the sidewalk. A couple passed under the streetlight, faces glowing.

I typed in one of the addresses that Henri had provided and within seconds, I was hooked. Two hours passed as I perused websites, reading about the golden age of Hollywood and the world of movie poster collecting.

At midnight I finally pulled myself away, shutting down the computer and inserting Henri's notes into a folder to take it with me. I hurried back into the waiting room, hit the light switch and locked the hall door.

As I walked back to the elevator, my jeans made a swishing sound. Whoosh. Whoosh. Whoosh. In the stillness, it sounded like a chainsaw being revved up.

I hit the elevator button and the doors slid open. I was about the get on when I stopped. Was I going to let a little paranoia scare me out of my usual routine of taking the stairs? You bet.

I got in and rode down to the first floor, laughing at myself for being such a weenie. Some detective I am. Maybe if I carried my gun instead of just practicing with it, I would feel better.

The doors eased open and I stepped out.

A faint whistling sound broke the stillness and then my brain exploded. A million stars created a hazy colored pattern in my vision. My legs buckled, and I dropped the folder. I went down with twin thoughts circling in my head. One: Duck before the next blow comes. And two: This couldn't be happening to me again.

My knees hit the floor and I tucked and rolled, sprawling into the lobby. A piece of 2x4 slammed down with a crack, narrowly missing my head. Wood chips flew past my cheeks.

I ended up on all fours, but quickly got my feet under me. My attacker had on dark clothes, gloves, and a black ski mask. He raised the wood again, holding it over his head like a pick axe. I launched myself upward, my right shoulder hitting him squarely in the stomach.

"Ugh," a low voice gasped. The 2x4 fell to the floor with a clatter.

We collapsed like two bowling pins, kicking and tumbling over each other. I ended up on top of him, using my torso to pin him under me. He squirmed, but I was able to land a glancing strike off the side of his face. At the same time, his fists flayed out, darting around my face and upper body. A punch connected squarely on my chin. My teeth clanked together, jolting me all the way in my toes. The colored stars returned as I fell off of him, landing on my back with my legs twisted beneath me.

The attacker pounced on me and pummeled me with vicious blows. It was all I could do to ward him off. In a desperate attempt to stop him, I thrust my hands out. I grabbed his throat and squeezed for all I was worth. The pounding stopped and he grabbed my wrists, yanking my hands from his neck.

Agile as a monkey, he bounced to his feet. I rolled to one side, sucking wind. A black boot with a steel tip kicked me in the ribs. A searing pain ripped through me, like I'd been stabbed. I gasped for breath, couldn't get any. Before I could move, he grabbed the 2x4 and whacked me in the back. If I thought I couldn't get breath before, it was worse now.

I desperately tried to get oxygen as the man hefted the board again. My ribs and back screamed in pain and I barely managed to lift an arm to ward off another blow. My attacker clutched the board like a baseball bat and was about to use me as the ball when he hesitated. He stared out the front doors, then suddenly whirled around. He stooped to the floor and grabbed my file. Just like that, he disappeared around the corner.

I lay helplessly on the floor, my breathing ragged. After an eternity I pulled myself into a ball, scooting on my butt until I could lean back against the wall. Each breath caused a firestorm on my right side. I huddled on the floor, too tired and too hurt to move. I didn't know where my attacker was, and at that moment, I didn't care. If he came back to finish the job, at least the pain would stop.

After a bit, I acclimated to the sharp jabs in my side, panting in little breaths so my ribs didn't expand too much. My head throbbed, and the left side of my scalp felt wet. I touched my cheek and stared at my hand. Blood. It looked like chocolate syrup in the darkness. I touched my head and found a gash above my left ear. It was oozing blood through my hair and down the left side of my face.

As I gazed at my hand, at the blood – my blood – anger rose in me like bile. So did my desire to live. I didn't know what had scared my attacker away, but I wouldn't be here if he came back. I slowly pushed myself up the wall until I was standing. I tested my legs. They supported my weight. My ribs and head I wasn't so sure of.

I took a tentative step and felt woozy, but I cautiously made my way to the building entrance, bent over like Quasimodo. I favored my right side as I shambled outside and down the sidewalk to the parking lot. I fully expected to run into someone, but thankfully no one saw me. I rounded the corner and snuck between the cars to the second row.

The 4-Runner sat near the end and even in my foggy state I could see that something was amiss. As I approached my car, I saw glass sprinkled around the front end. Someone, gee I wonder who, had bashed both headlights to smithereens. I shouldn't have been shocked, but I was.

I stared at the place where a light bulb should have been, wheezing, trying to ignore the stinging in my side. Laughter drifted toward me from the street, interrupting my reverie. I lifted my eyes to the front windshield. A crackling pattern covered the passenger side window.

I cursed as I dug my keys out of my pocket. I traipsed around the side of the 4-Runner, checking for further damage. The taillights had received the same treatment as the headlights. Red pieces of plastic floated in a muddy puddle. I stepped over the puddle and tripped, landing in a heap beside the car next to mine. A thousand pieces of light shimmered across my vision as a thousand tiny volts of pain hit me from various points in my body.

"Hey mister, are you okay?"

I wasn't sure the voice was real. I shakily stood up and fought a wave of nausea as I angrily scanned the ground and saw what had tripped me. A piece of 2x4 approximately three feet long lay half in the puddle. I picked it up. Amongst the dirt and rainwater on the wood, I saw flecks of blood. I unlocked the car and hurled the two-by-four onto the back seat. Not that I would find any fingerprints or anything on it. As evidence, it was useless. As motivation, it was priceless.

"Oh my gosh, Mark! He's hurt."

I turned from the car and stared at a middle-aged man and who I assumed was his wife. They stared back at me, their faces a mix of concern and horror. Mark slowly moved towards me, his wife clinging to his elbow.

"Did someone attack you?" Mark asked. His voice sounded far off.

I nodded mutely. I didn't want to say so, but Mark and his wife didn't look so good. They were both out of focus, hazy at the edges. I grabbed Mark's arm. "You look terrible," I said. He frowned at me.

"Call an ambulance," Mark said.

Good idea. He needed one.

The wife pulled a cell phone from her purse.

"No," I mumbled, shakier with each movement. "I'll be fine. I just need to sit down."

Mark's face twisted into a Picasso painting. Suddenly I was on the ground, not sure how I got there. The voices faded and I blacked out.

# CHAPTER FIFTEEN

The bright lights hurt my eyes. The sight of Willie Rhoden did not.

"What happened to you?" she asked, concern etched on her face.

"What are you doing here?" I asked, not knowing where 'here' was. I turned my head to one side, instantly regretting the movement. A dull throb pulsed behind my eyes. An oxygen tube poked up under my nostrils, and something warmed on my brow. "Where is here?" I asked, scrunching my eyes shut.

"You're at Denver Health," Willie said, laying a gloved hand on my forehead. "An ambulance brought you in a while ago. Seems like a nice couple saw you pass out and they called for help."

That explained how I ended up at the hospital.

"What time is it?" Wasn't it night? I gazed at Willie. "What are you doing here?" I repeated. She usually worked at Saint Joseph's Hospital, at the front desk.

"I'm moonlighting here." She pursed her lips as she daubed a piece of gauze on my head. "Reed, what happened to you? You've got a gash the size of Texas over your ear, and your face looks like a bruised banana."

A fog surrounded my brain. I shut my eyes, but I couldn't remember what had happened.

"I went to the office," I said. "But I don't remember why. I remember seeing stars. Pretty ones, blue, green, orange. A man skiing, you know, with a black mask that covered his whole face. And the parking lot. I remember the parking lot," I said triumphantly.

Willie looked at me like I'd lost more than a little blood. "You probably have a concussion. That can affect your short-term memory."

"Someone assaulted me," I concluded, as any great detective would. As I talked, I became aware of my side hurting.

She gave me a no-shit-Sherlock look. "Who?"

I opened my eyes, squinting at Willie. "I don't know, but I intend to find out."

She worked on the side of my head, cleaning out the cut. I gritted my teeth and focused on something other than my body hurting. My attacker was male. Either that or a very masculine female, a la the 1970's East German athletes. The last thing I remembered clearly was playing pool with the Goofball Brothers. That was it.

"They need to take some X-rays," Willie said, breaking me away from my thoughts.

For the next hour I endured a series of tests that determined that I indeed had a concussion, along with two broken ribs and a bruised back, but no damage to my lungs or kidneys. I received eight stitches on my scalp, complete with the obligatory shave around the wound area. The rest of my hair wasn't long enough to cover the wound, so that part of my anatomy looked akin to the Frankenstein monster's head. I had a black smudge under my left eye, a couple of other small bruises on my cheeks, and a tiny cut on my chin that required nothing more than a Band-Aid. Now I just wanted a lollipop and my own home.

"Here's your insurance forms," Willie said. I leaned on the bed in one of the emergency room cubicles. As Willie helped me ease back into my shirt, she did a first-class job of avoiding eye contact. "They need you to sign a release form out front. I called a taxi for you."

"Hey, what's wrong? I'm the one who's hurt."

Willie stared at the floor. I tilted her chin up and gazed into wet emeralds as tears formed at the corners of her eyes.

"What?"

"This is exactly what I was talking about," she said, her lower lip quivering. "What if we started going out and something happens to you? Something worse than this?"

"I could get hit by a bus, too. We take risks every time we go out our front doors. As a matter of fact, our own homes are more dangerous than a lot of places."

She sniffled. "You're not funny."

"I'm not trying to be."

She jerked her head away, and grabbed a clipboard off the end of the bed. "My father was a cop, Reed. When I was little, I worried what might happen to him. Every day he left for work, I didn't know if he would come home. It's a terrible way to live, the not knowing."

Without turning around, she squared her shoulders and scurried out of the room.

» » » » »

Something squawked. I rolled over and immediately regretted it. A gray filter of light oozed in between the cracks in the blinds. Rain pattered lightly on the roof.

Damn birds, I thought. Don't they know only Gene Kelly sings in the rain?

The squawk sounded again, only shriller. This time I diagnosed the noise correctly.

"Hello?" I said, picking up the phone from the nightstand.

"Hello, dear." My mother's high-pitched voice carried over the phone lines like a parrot on cocaine. "You sound groggy. Why is it every time I call, you're asleep? Does this have something to do with that detective work? Are you on drugs? Paul," she yelled away from the phone, "your son's on drugs, I just know it."

My mother's worst fear, other than the fact that I might not marry and produce offspring, was that I was secretly doing drugs. It didn't help that I'd never had a history of drug or alcohol problems, nor that my worst experience with illicit chemicals occurred more than ten years ago in college, when Cal and I bought a package of tortillas smothered in flour and wrapped in foil from a man on the street, thinking we'd purchased a brick of Columbia's finest. And how she always managed to call right after I'd had some kind of mishap, I'll never know.

"I'm not on drugs, Mother." Except for some pain medication, and that came from the emergency room doctor. I had left Denver Health in a taxi with enough pain pills to last until I could get a prescription filled. Once I got home, I woke up the Goofball Brothers, explaining my predicament – I had a concussion and needed to be monitored. After some haggling, they decided that Deuce would stay with me through the night, and then Ace would check on me in the morning, and then both would periodically come by to see me, as their schedules permitted. I dozed on the couch and Ace woke me every two hours throughout the remainder of the night, following the instructions I was given for treating the concussion. The next morning, Deuce filled my prescription once the pharmacy opened. Each brother checked on me a couple of times, both in person and over the phone. The last time, when Deuce came, we decided that I was doing better, and I crawled gratefully into bed and let sleep take me. Until the phone rang.

"What time is it?" I mumbled to my mother.

"It's six o'clock. I called you yesterday at the office, and again last night at home. Deuce answered and said you were taking a nap. He's such a nice boy. All of the Smith boys are nice, now that you mention it." I hadn't mentioned it, but didn't bother to say so. "Deuce said he would leave you a note. I think it's terribly rude of you to not call me back, Reed. I didn't raise you to act that way..."

"What time is it?" I asked again. I swung my legs over the side of the bed and sat up, immediately aware of dull pain throughout my body.

"I told you, it's six o'clock, dear."

That meant it was four o'clock in Colorado. "What day?"

"What?" She huffed into the phone. "Why, it's Sunday. Reed, what is going on?"

I stared at my toes. I'd been asleep, or out of it, for more than a day. And I still felt groggy.

"Reed?" my mother chirped. "Paul, find out what's wrong."

"Wait, Mom..." I said into the receiver, but was too late. My father's gruff voice came on.

"Son, look what you've done. Your mother's in a panic now, and you know I'll never hear the end of it."

"I'm fine, Dad," I said, and proceeded to explain that I'd encountered some minor trouble with the case I was working on. I left out my meeting with a man in a ski mask and the trip to the hospital.

"Don't know why you can't get a decent job," he said. I pictured him in his khaki shorts and polo shirt, sitting on the deck of their ritzy south Florida condo, overlooking the ocean, with his neatly trimmed salt-

and-pepper hair gelled into place, and his gold jewelry and Rolex watch glinting in the late afternoon sun. The model of respectability and wealth. And here I was, tarnishing the family name and money in my quest for independence.

I sighed heavily and gingerly put a hand to my side. Little breaths, I told myself.

"I like what I'm doing," I said. "It beats going to work in a suit and tie every day."

"I know, son. As long as you're happy," he said halfheartedly. I'd been doing the detective gig for over a year, and I knew my father secretly hoped that it was a passing fancy, like many of the other jobs I'd had since college. But since my grandparents left me some money, I could be choosy about what I did and how much money I needed to make.

We did the small-talk routine for a couple of minutes. "Tell Mom I'm okay, and I'll call her in a few days," I said when I could tell that he'd covered all his bases.

I hung up the phone and cautiously stood up. Once the stars subsided, I plodded to the bathroom where I surveyed myself in the mirror. My left eye was purple with a tinge of yellow around the edges, and the other bruises on my face looked like smudges of charcoal. My hair stuck out in all directions, and the stitches looked like a black ladder running along my head. The band-aid on my chin appeared the least threatening.

I shuffled into the kitchen and made a PB&J, poured a cold glass of milk and took them to the living room. I ate slowly while I checked my phone messages. Three were from the Goofball Brothers, checking in and wondering how I could sleep so soundly. One from Cal, asking me to call him, no reason. One from Bob, inquiring if I was okay, and that he was available if I needed anything. A message from Jack was next, asking about progress in the case. Then Willie, wondering how I was doing, and that she was sorry she'd gotten upset with me the other night, but that she hoped I would understand her feelings. And finally Henri Benoit, asking me if I'd gotten the notes he had left at the office.

What notes? I had to think back until I remembered that I had talked to Henri the other night. I was at B 52's and he said he would leave notes about *The Maltese Falcon* poster under the door. I looked around the room but didn't see anything. I wondered if I had left them at the office.

I put the phone down and finished my sandwich. I'd lost a day on an investigation that was going nowhere, I'd scared Willie off, and I'd gotten my ass kicked. I finished off the glass of milk and leaned back, dozing.

Who was I threatening? That question popped into my brain as I awoke with a start. The empty milk glass lay on the carpet, where I had dropped it.

I set the glass on the coffee table and picked up a pen and paper to jot down some of my thoughts when I spied the note.

"Dude," it read. "We watched the house like you asked. Deuce saw a man go in with a black bag yesterday around lunchtime. I didn't see anyone last night, but maybe there was a light on in the back window. I got scared and left. Sorry. Bob says to call us when you get up." Deuce's scrawled signature was at the bottom of the page. Underneath that: "P. S. – We got your car yesterday and took it to the shop. It should be ready in a day or two." For a Goofball Brother, this was practically a novel.

I sat back and shut my eyes. On top of everything else, the 4-

Runner had been vandalized. I'd forgotten that piece, but I must've told the Brothers about it. They were doing a good job of watching over me. I owed them plenty.

I read through the note again. There was a lot of activity at the house on Madison Avenue. I wondered if the owners were doing some remodeling before it sold. But didn't Edna Mills tell me that she just wanted to be rid of the place? Maybe she had to repair a few things in order for that to happen.

My files for the house on 210 Madison were at the office, but I got lucky and found Edna's number online. The clock on the wall said it was 5:30. I hoped that Edna was enjoying a Sunday evening at home.

She picked up on the third ring.

"Oh, the man interested in the architecture of the house," she said after I identified myself.

We exchanged a few pleasantries, and then I asked her about repairs to the house.

"We're taking care of some stuff," she answered. "Even though our price was so low, there were a few things this couple asked to be changed, and they weren't all the big items like that young man wanted. My husband said we should turn them down and wait for the next buyer and we wouldn't have to hassle with contractors and whatnot, but the buyers are such a nice couple, you see. I couldn't bring myself to do that to them. And I didn't want to go through finding another buyer, after all. We do want to finish all this and move on."

I thanked her for her time and hung up. That explained the activity at the house. And it meant I was barking up the wrong tree. But I was closing in on someone, or I wouldn't have been assaulted.

I grabbed the phone again and hit autodial. Ace picked up on the third ring.

"Reed, how's it going?"

"Better," I said, even though I didn't really believe it.

"Did you get our note? Bob said not to worry about your car. He'll make sure it gets fixed, and let you know when it's ready."

"Thanks. I appreciate his help. And you guys, too."

"No problem. Hey, you want to have dinner with us?"

"I just ate, but thanks."

"You still want someone watching that house?"

"No. You guys did a great job, but I don't need you there anymore."

"Okay." Ace sounded relieved. "That place is spooky."

"It's probably just someone doing repairs. Thanks for your help."

"Deuce wants to know when he can carry a gun."

"Tell him when he gets his detective license, we'll talk." You didn't need a license to be a detective in Colorado, but I knew Deuce would never discover this. He'd worry that he would have to take a test to get a license, and that would be enough to deter him.

Ace hollered my answer to Deuce as I hung up.

Next, I called Willie but she wasn't home or wasn't answering the phone. I left a message, thanking her for her kind treatment at the hospital – leaving out any snide remarks about walking out on me – and I let her know that I was home and recuperating okay. I said if she wanted, she could come over for a while.

I got up and looked around the house but didn't find any notes from Henri. His notes were either at the office, or I must have dropped them during the attack. I couldn't remember anything right before or after I was assaulted. The emergency room doctor had informed me that this was a common occurrence after sustaining a concussion, but it didn't help the frustration I felt of not knowing what happened.

I didn't have any energy left so I eased back onto the couch and watched part of *The Killers*, an apt choice given my investigation. The 1946 movie was based on a short story by Ernest Hemingway. It had plenty of deception, dark characters, and a femme fatale, but even with all that I fell asleep halfway through. At midnight I awoke just long enough to realize that Willie never called. In a semi-stupor, I turned off the television and sprawled into bed.

# CHAPTER SIXTEEN

"Try the burritos," I said. "They're to die for."

Cal took my suggestion and ordered one, along with a Sprite.

It was noon on Monday, and Cal and I were having lunch at Josephina's, a hip hole-in-the-wall Mexican restaurant a few blocks from my condo.

The waitress, an attractive brunette with piercing brown eyes, threw me a funny look when she saw my black eye. In the three days since the attack, the flesh around my left eye had morphed into a lovely shade of deep purple, and the other bruises that showed resembled an old banana. She barely made eye contact as she took my order, but smiled seductively at Cal as she jotted down his order. She followed the smile with a wink before sauntering away.

"She's flirting with you," I said.

"Huh?" Cal swiveled in his seat, eyeing the waitress as she disappeared into the kitchen. "You think so?" He turned back around and shrugged at me.

I rolled my eyes at him. Clueless. "I want everything you can get on Samantha Healy," I said, changing the subject. "I called Jack Healy earlier to give him a status report, and I found out her maiden name is Simpson."

Cal, the man who rarely leaves his house, had made an exception for his wounded friend. Since my 4-Runner wouldn't be fixed until late in the day, and because I was still feeling stiff and sore, Cal had offered to take me to lunch, then over to Henri's shop to get a new set of notes about *The Maltese Falcon* poster.

Earlier that morning, I returned several phone calls. Jack had been surprised and concerned that I'd been assaulted. The maintenance crew of my office building hadn't known about the door lock mechanism being jammed until yesterday. They had fixed it, explaining that a nail had been shoved into the slot, disabling the lock and the door. No one had turned in any paperwork from Henri Benoit. Then I had called Henri. After explaining what had happened and enduring a torrent of sympathies in French, we'd arranged to meet at his office after lunch.

"Samantha's the ex-wife?" Cal asked.

"Right. And the logical person to kill Ned."

The waitress returned with our drinks. She took extra care to eye Cal again. He remained unbelievably clueless. I took a big gulp of soda.

"Why didn't the police suspect Samantha?" Cal asked.

"There was no reason to," I said. "I called the insurance company earlier today, and they said that the policy should have been taken care of, but because Ned moved, they had some clerical errors, and it wasn't until recently that they even knew he had died. At that point they had to fulfill the policy."

"Who informed the insurance company that he died?"

"An anonymous phone call. From a woman."

Cal cocked one eyebrow. "An anonymous woman? That's what the insurance people said?"

"Scout's honor." I held up three fingers in the Boy Scout salute.

"If Samantha knew about the policy, she could've called and got the ball rolling."

"But why wait to kill him? It could've given Ned time to change the name on the policy, or cancel it."

"I don't know. Maybe she just found out that her name was still on the policy, so that's when she acted."

"Here you go, sport," the waitress said as she set Cal's plate down. Being called 'sport' would've turned me off, but it didn't do a thing for Cal. A hint of disappointment crossed her face as she laid my plate down. I smiled as she flounced off.

I devoured my burrito. It was the best meal I'd had in days, given that I'd been laid up since Friday. Now if my ribs would quit hurting and I could get rid of the headache, I'd be fine.

"How would Samantha find out that her name was still on the policy?" Cal asked.

"I don't know," I said as I loaded up a tortilla chip with salsa. "Maybe Ned said something. Samantha said she talked to Ned before he died, and that he told her things would be different. Maybe he mentioned the policy then. Or she could've checked on her own by calling the insurance company."

"Why would Ned tell her that? If he did."

"If I knew that, I wouldn't be asking you for help." Cal shrugged off my jab at him. "There's something about Samantha that I can't place," I said, sliding back on the vinyl seat. "Something doesn't fit."

Cal finished his lunch and pushed his plate away. "And I won't ask what, because then you wouldn't need me."

"Very funny," I smirked.

"Who mugged you the other night?"

"I don't know. I don't remember much right before or after I got hit. But Samantha could've set me up. She could've been following me, and planned the whole thing."

"What about her alibi for the night Ned was killed?"

"I haven't had a chance to check anything out, but I'll see what I can find out after we see Henri."

"Speaking of Henri…" Cal looked at his watch. "We should get going."

I dropped some bills on the table as we left. Our waitress was nowhere in sight, saving Cal from one last flirtatious run-in with her. Not that he was aware of any of it.

» » » » »

The drizzly rain of yesterday had swept further east, and the sun was beating down on the city again. As we drove down Broadway I was thankful for the bright rays, as it gave me an excuse to wear dark sunglasses without looking funny. I would be exceedingly glad when my black eye went away, along with the stares. Cal parked on a side street and we walked down a block to Classic Hollywood Memorabilia.

As we stepped inside, a bell over the door chimed. Henri Benoit limped over to greet us.

"Ah, Reed, let me get a look at you," he said, pursing his lips and nodding his head in sympathy. "This is just terrible, eh? Why would someone do this to you?"

I was tempted to show Henri my side, where I'd been kicked in the ribs. The bruise there was the size of a football with similar coloration. I had another nice bruise along my back, too, but I didn't think Henri would want to see that one either.

"And look at your head." Henri situated his bifocals on the tip of his nose and peered up at my scalp, where the hair around the black stitches had grown to the length of peach fuzz. I wanted to wear a hat, but when I attempted to put one on, the brim of the cap rested right over the stitches, irritating them, so I chose to go bareheaded and endure the stares. I planned on a trip to the barber soon, to even out the hair above both ears, but in the meantime I could only hope the wound made me look tough, because I wasn't getting any other payoff from my injuries.

"He's a charmer," Cal said with a lopsided grin.

I introduced Cal to Henri as we followed Henri to the back of the shop.

"I have the notes I gave you saved on the computer," Henri said, limping around the counter. He perched on the edge of a stool and manipulated the mouse, and in seconds, a printer next to the monitor spat out some paper.

"Here you go," Henri handed them to me.

"What's the big deal with this stuff?" Cal asked. His eyes roved around the store, scanning all the items for sale.

"You are not a collector, eh?"

Cal shook his head.

"Ah, that is too bad." Henri moved around the counter to a display case containing small props from a variety of movies. "There is much history in all this stuff." He pointed to a tiny set of white gloves on a shelf. "You see these? Vivian Leigh wore those gloves during the shooting of *Gone with the Wind*. And this pair of boots," he tapped on the glass. "They belonged to John Wayne."

Cal leaned down and studied the memorabilia. "Okay."

"Okay." Henri threw up his hands at me. "What is this, 'okay'?" Henri turned to me. "Your friend does not have a passion for art, eh? No sense of history?"

Cal reddened. "I know history, just not about Hollywood."

Henri patted Cal on the arm. "It is okay, as you say. We all place our passions in different areas, eh?"

Cal eyed the price tag on an autographed picture of Frank Sinatra. "So people really pay big money for this stuff?"

Henri waggled his head enthusiastically. "Of course. Many collectors spend millions on their collections."

"Millions?" Cal asked. "What could sell for that much?"

"Not all things are that expensive, but take Reed's poster for instance. If it is real, it could be worth twelve to fifteen thousand dollars."

"For a piece of paper?"

Henri shook his head in despair – his pupil was not getting it. I stood back and watched the show.

"It is part of history, part of our culture, yes? So many films have influenced our lives, and the actors did, too. Films gave people a way of escape during the Great Depression. Charlie Chaplin, the Marx Brothers, they made people laugh; John Wayne defined the macho male. Mae West, Joan Crawford, Bette Davis charmed men, and helped establish fashion trends, just like the actors of today do. Many of those actors helped the war effort during the '40's. Look at Mickey Mouse and the whole Disney phenomena, how that mouse became a part of our culture. The list is endless. These posters are a part of our past, just like the costumes, the props, and all the other stuff, as you call it."

Cal's face was blank. If it wasn't about computers, he probably wasn't interested. I, on the other hand, could appreciate. I was practically drooling with every word Henri said.

"But even if you pay ten thousand for something," Cal said, "you'd have to buy an awful lot of posters to hit the million mark."

"Ah, but it isn't just posters. It's autographs, props, clothing worn by the actors. And the rarer something is, the more valuable it becomes. In the early days of film, many studios produced their own posters, as well as window and lobby cards, for their movies, then distributed these with the films. The same posters and cards would be reused from theater to theater, leaving the posters worn. Because of that, many films do not have associated posters or cards anymore."

"Wait a minute," Cal said. "I remember seeing something on TV about a house in the Midwest. The owners were renovating and they tore down some walls, and a bunch of posters had been used in the walls as insulation."

"I remember hearing about that," I said.

"Ah, yes," Henri smiled. "I believe they found a lobby card from a Bette Davis movie, the only one in existence. How do you put a price on that?"

Cal shrugged, but he was interested.

"That's a fun story, yes? But it shows you how a rare item can become worth so much. There have been more than a few cases of people finding posters in their walls, or in old frames. The Bette Davis lobby card was produced in the thirties, when the studios still produced the cards. After 1940, the National Screen Service was formed, taking on the responsibility of numbering posters, and creating more quantities for theaters. Which is why a pre-1940 poster is usually a much rarer find."

"Too bad my poster wasn't made before then," I said.

"If it is an original," Henri said.

Cal's eyes widened. "If it looks old, why wouldn't it be an

original?"

"Ah, there are many forgers who are crafty about making a poster appear old, much like an original."

"And they do that because collecting is big business," Cal said to Henri, who beamed. His student was catching on.

"Don't Academy Awards sell for a lot?" I asked.

"Ah, the Oscar," Henri said with a thoughtful nod. "This is true. Technically the Academy of Motion Picture Arts and Sciences has the right to buy an Oscar back, but they are auctioned off anyway. Steven Spielberg has bought two Oscars at auction. He paid over $500,000 for Clark Gable's Oscar for *It Happened One Night*, and more than that for Bette Davis' Oscar from *Jezebel*, and then he returned them both to the Academy. But many private collectors own Oscars. Did you know Michael Jackson bought producer David O. Selznick's Best Picture Oscar for *Gone with the Wind?*" Cal shook his head, but I nodded assent. This was all right up my alley. "An Oscar is a prized piece for a collector," Henri finished.

"But expensive," I said.

"And now you know why millions can be spent on a collection," Henri said to Cal. "There was one collector I met when I had a shop in New York, Frank Gray, who had a beautiful collection of memorabilia. He spent years amassing all kinds of items. He owned at least a couple of Oscar statuettes. Now, he had bought his items years ago, when the prices weren't as high, and people were not collecting like they are now. And Frank was rumored to have a very exceptional piece."

"What's that?" I asked.

"You've heard of Barry Fitzgerald? The actor?"

"Sure." I nodded. "He won a Best Supporting Oscar for *Going My*

*Way* in 1944."

"Right, but do you know why that Oscar was unique?"

"Barry beheaded it while playing golf in his house."

"Correct."

"How could you damage an Oscar like that?" Cal asked. "Aren't they made of metal?"

Henri launched into a description of wartime Oscars. "Because of the need for precious metals during World War II, the statuettes during that time were made of plaster."

"And after the war, Oscar winners turned the plaster ones in and got the traditional bronze with gold-plate replacements," I said.

Henri's smile got even brighter at my knowledge of Oscar trivia.

"But since Barry had damaged his plaster one, the Academy issued a replacement for it," I continued. "Then after the war, he turned in the plaster statuette and got a gold one."

"And what happened to the beheaded statuette?" Henri asked.

"I assume it was destroyed," I said.

He smiled. "And that's where the rumors start, eh?"

I waited for him to continue. Cal was hooked. He was staring intently at Henri.

"For many years, people heard that Barry Fitzgerald's original Oscar, the beheaded one, was not destroyed, but kept by a member of the Academy. Over time it was lost but Frank was rumored to have found it in an antique store in Hollywood."

"Something that rare and unique must be worth a fortune," Cal said.

Henri nodded. "If the rumor were true, then yes."

"It's not true?" Cal and I both asked at once.

Henri smiled. "The award may not have been destroyed, that I cannot say. But I can say for certain that Frank owned only a replica of the beheaded Oscar, not the original headless statuette."

"How do you know that?"

"He told me himself how his wife had hired an artist to make a headless statuette for him as a joke. However, the artist made one small mistake in replicating the statue."

"What mistake?"

Henri smiled. "Oscar statues stand on a movie reel. But the artist intentionally changed the design of the reel." Henri looked at me and winked. "You would know the difference. But it still gave Frank a lot of pleasure to have the replica in his collection."

The chimes above the door rang. We looked up as a heavyset woman entered the store.

"Ah, it is fun to digress, but now it is time to work." Henri stripped off his glasses and bowed his head slightly. "Reed, I will analyze your poster soon, and we shall see if it is indeed more than "stuff"."

Cal smiled at the joke. "I'm sure Reed hopes it's an original."

"Absolutely," I said, grinning. "I'll take a look at these." I held up Henri's notes.

"Good," Henri said, leaving us to help his customer.

# CHAPTER SEVENTEEN

"How ya feeling?" Cal asked me.

It was later in the evening, and Cal was sitting at a small mahogany desk in my home office, my favorite place in the condo. I am an incurable collector, and I love to work in the office surrounded by all the collections I have painstakingly acquired. Floor-to-ceiling bookshelves on one wall hold some of my favorite books, mostly murder mysteries, some great pictures from a memorable trip to Europe, and a collection of rare first-edition detective novels. A storage case is filled with my favorite detective movies, along with a collection of Alfred Hitchcock classics. But the thing I like best about the room is the glass display case in the corner of the room that has a first edition of *A Study in Scarlet*, by Sir Alfred Conan Doyle.

I was stretched out on a brown leather loveseat, which was a new addition to the room.

"I'm fine," I said as I stared up at the ceiling. "Just tired."

As the sun set, a weak purple light filtered through the window, and the room became a series of dim shadows. My eyelids began to sag as I struggled to stay awake.

"This shouldn't take too long," Cal said.

I squinted at him. Brilliant white light from the computer monitor made his 5 o'clock shadow seem eerie, as if his jaw was covered in silt, but he was more at ease in front of the computer than he'd been all day helping me run errands.

We had stopped at a barber and I endured the stares while a young woman barely out of her teens evened out my hair around the stitches. She cropped my hair on the sides and left a dollop of curly hair on top. I looked like a Marine. I couldn't wait for next week, when I would get the stitches out – at least people would stop looking at my head. Cal had ribbed me relentlessly about my haircut as we stopped by my office to check messages and get the mail. Finally, at close to six, I was able to pick up the 4-Runner. The manager of the shop was close friends with Bob Smith, so the shop fixed the car in record time.

Throughout the day, Cal had been doing such a good job of mingling amongst the human race that I didn't hear a complaint from him until we arrived back at my condo. A tenacious elderly lady whose car was blocking my street finally sent him over the edge. He honked the horn loudly at her, then glared in her direction as she finally maneuvered her car on down the street.

Safely back in my condo, we had ordered a pizza, and after devouring it, we'd begun the research on Samantha Healy. To be accurate, Cal was researching. I hadn't lifted a finger, and I didn't intend to. I wanted to sleep. But Cal couldn't keep away from the computer, settling comfortably back into his virtual world.

I closed my eyes, checking my eyelids for holes. None so far.

"Ah-ha!"

"What?" I turned on my side and faced the desk, tucking my arms under my head.

"I found Samantha's acting class."

"Duh. I gave you the name of the school and the class. It couldn't have been that hard."

Cal threw a pencil at me. "Denver Alternative College. *A good place to know when you're on the go.*"

"What's that, their slogan?"

"You got it. Man, this is like the community college's community college. Where the nobodies go." Cal's bad one-liners continued as the mouse clicked.

"That's terrible," I said.

"I'm just kidding. Let's see," he mumbled to himself. "Acting classes, here we go." Click.

"So are these acting classes for the off-off-off-off Broadway actors?"

Cal chuckled. "The class Samantha was enrolled in finished at the end of June, but there's another class going on now with the same instructor. She might be able to verify Samantha's alibi."

"Uh-huh." I didn't have the energy to move.

"And lucky you, the class meets tomorrow night."

I shut my eyes.

"Let me write this down for you." Papers shuffling. "What's this?"

I cracked one eye open. Cal was peering at a notepad on the table. "Doing some research on the Internet? Taking my job away?"

I tilted my head up. "That was Ned Healy's. I used it when I went to his house. Those must be his notes."

"The great detective misses nothing," Cal said with a heavy dose of sarcasm.

"Yeah, how his client was able to use the Internet." I yawned and closed my eyes. Cal's laughter sounded like it was filtered through a tunnel, and I was vaguely aware of him leaving the room before I fell asleep.

» » » » »

The next morning, I noticed that the soreness was ebbing slightly. That, combined with having my car back from the mechanic's rather than relying on Cal, had me in a jubilant mood. Cal was my best friend, but a little of him went a long way.

The smell of cheap Mexican food and wet wood assaulted me as I walked into Denver Alternative College, a two-story cinder-block building on East Colfax Avenue, a mile down the road from the gold-domed State Capitol. Yellow brick walls down the main entryway made me feel like I was walking through a tunnel painted honey gold. A few students roamed the halls. Most were dressed in business casual, presumably because they'd just come from their day jobs and were now ready to improve themselves through night classes.

I glanced at the notepad with the course information that Cal had written down last night. "The Art of Acting" was being held in room 103-A at seven o'clock. I was a half-hour early, and I hoped to find the instructor before the students arrived.

I made my way past a bulletin board covered in a kaleidoscope of papers and post-it notes advertising everything from job openings to party announcements. At the end of the hall, I descended six stairs down to a lower level, and, at the end of a short corridor, found 103-A.

I peeked through a thin rectangle window into an auditorium classroom with a large stage and ten rows of wooden chairs perched on an easy slope toward the back of the room. The auditorium was empty.

I eased the door open and slipped in, letting my eyes adjust to soft lighting coming from somewhere offstage. The rest of the room remained in deep shadows.

I was about to walk down an aisle on the left when the door opened behind me. I heard a loud click and bright lights immediately illuminated the room. I turned to see a shriveled woman in baggy turquoise pants, a flowing cream-colored silk shirt, stiletto heels a hideous shade of aqua, and an embarrassing amount of makeup.

"May I help you?" she asked, her voice like an electric razor.

"I'm looking for Xania Diviny," I said, pronouncing the name "Zania". I stared at her eyelashes, which seemed as long as my pinky fingers.

"Ex-ZAY-nee-ah." She corrected. She held up a wrinkled and age-spotted hand, palm down, as if she wanted me to bow and kiss it. "Di-VIN-i-tee."

"Excuse me?"

"It's Divinity. Xania Divinity." That's what I get for relying on Cal's scribbled notes. "What can I do for you?"

I took her hand and shook it, giving her my best smile. She ran her eyes over me, then let her hand drop disappointedly to her side.

"You don't look like an actor. You have poor posture, your eyes are too hard, your haircut is hideous, and your smile is nothing short of goofy." So much for my charm. "I couldn't possibly work with so little."

"That's good," I said, "since I'm not interested in acting classes."

"Oh?" She took a step back, hand now on her chest, still surveying me. "I'm glad you see the futility of this."

I stepped back too, leaning on the back of the wooden theater seats.

"I'd like to ask you a few questions about a student of yours."

"And who might that be?"

"Samantha Healy."

"What do you want to know about her?"

I pulled out a business card from my wallet and handed it to her. Xania jerked as if I'd struck her. She now put her hand to her throat in what I could only guess was intended as a melodramatic pose, but the numerous silver and turquoise bracelets dangling from her wrist robbed the gesture of any real meaning.

"You're a detective, Mr. – " She glanced at the card. "Mr....Reed." I guess Ferguson was too hard to read, or pronounce. "Is Samantha in some kind of trouble?"

"Samantha said she was in your class, Actors and Acting, last semester," I said, ignoring the question.

"Yes, that's true. She has been a student of mine for a few years."

"I noticed that the school catalog shows the class is three hours long."

Xania pursed her lips, then sucked a breath in through a slit and let it slowly out. "When you have so little to work with, you need a lot of time."

"Samantha isn't a good actress?"

"Most of my students have a lot of learning to do. That's why they're here. Samantha makes progress, but it will be some time before she will be cast in the student audition play."

"The what?"

"The student audition play." Xania frowned at me, and her rouge cracked into tiny red wrinkle lines. "At the end of each semester, our more experienced students audition for roles in a play that we perform in front of the rest of the theater students. It gives the best of our actors a chance to refine their skills, and we invite local theater directors to the plays. This way the actors get exposure and the directors get a chance to informally audition new talent."

I feigned interest. "That sounds terrific."

"We have had great success with this. In all my years of instructing, I have had many pupils go on to great careers. You've heard of John Sayers?" I shook my head. "Anna Fredricks?" I shook my head again. "Darren Joyden?" I didn't bother this time. I figured the blank look on my face would be enough.

Xania clucked at my ignorance. "These actors were nothing, but I molded them so they were able to go on to grand things." Like what – billboards, underwear ads in the local papers, commercials on late-night cable?

"But Samantha isn't one of those," I said.

"If she keeps working with me, her acting will improve."

"Samantha said she was here on June 6th."

"Yes, that's true."

"How can you be so sure?" I asked, surprised that anyone could remember a seemingly random date pulled out of the air.

"We performed the student audition play for last semester that night." Xania put a gnarled hand on my elbow and guided me to a series of posters scotch-taped to the back wall. She pointed to a red poster with black letters, advertising the play "A Midsummer Night's Dream."

"Shakespeare," I said.

"We must all bow to the Bard if we want to ascend to greatness," Xania spoke with reverence.

Under the title was a list of actors, and then the line "One night only!" The date for the performance was June 6th, at 7:00 in the evening.

"But Samantha's name isn't here," I said. "Was she in some minor role?"

"She was not in the play, Reed," she said, her friendliness making me uncomfortable. "She is not at the level of these actors."

"Then…"

"Because," Xania interrupted me. "All enrolled students are required to attend the plays. It is an important part of an actor's development to study the performance of others." She pulled away from me and stood in a practiced pose. "This is why I teach. So others can learn from me, so they can benefit from my experience in theater and film."

In what, B-grade horror movies from the '50's?

"You remember seeing Samantha that night?"

"Of course." She gestured around the room. "The lights are on before the play starts. You can see everything, and I make it a point to note if a student misses my class. A lack of dedication is the ruin of any actor."

Before Xania could share more of her vast knowledge of herself, the rear door of the auditorium opened and a couple of students walked in, laughing and talking. When they saw Xania, they immediately straightened their postures and began whispering. They moved quietly to the front row and sat down, staring at the empty stage.

"Was the theater full for the performance?"

"Yes. We had a very talented group in the play, and the auditorium was full. We even had to bring in some extra chairs," she said proudly.

The door opened and more students shuffled in.

"As you can see, my class is about to begin." Xania surveyed me again. "Perhaps I have misjudged you. You have strong bones. Would you like to stay for a while and watch? We're rehearsing for our next play, *Romeo and Juliet.* You might find that you would want to work with me."

I accepted, but not because of Xania's flirting. I was dying to see how the class performed Shakespeare's classic.

At seven o'clock sharp, Xania began her class. I counted a total of twelve students, mostly young, and all in awe of Xania Divinity. Maybe she was a better actress and teacher than she was a dresser.

I slipped into a seat in the back row and watched Xania instruct the students in some techniques. She was actually quite good, her self-aggrandizing manner disappearing as she demonstrated various acting techniques.

After ten minutes, some of the actors assumed positions center stage, and the others sat in the front row seats. Xania settled into an end seat and stared up at the stage. Someone turned off the lights, plunging all but center stage into obscurity. Sitting nine rows back, I could barely make out the students in the front row.

I watched the first few lines of Act II, Scene 2, Romeo's speech to Juliet, in which he compares her to the sun. The acting wasn't bad, but when Juliet got to "Romeo, Romeo, wherefore art thou, Romeo", I grimaced. Juliet needed some work. If Samantha was worse than this, it was no wonder that she hadn't yet made it into a Spielberg movie. I stood up to go, eyeing Xania. She was intently watching the actors on stage, mouthing the lines as they spoke them. At least she knew her Shakespeare.

I tiptoed to the rear door and paused, turning back toward the stage. No one had noticed that I'd gotten up to leave, especially Xania. Her attention was riveted to the stage and the actors. The play had her full attention.

I eased out the door, watching to see if anyone noticed my leaving. All eyes were on Romeo and Juliet. No one turned when a sliver of light from the hallway penetrated the darkness.

As I walked up the stairs to the main hallway, I realized a few things. I'd never heard of Xania Divinity, but since I wasn't into B-grade horror movies, that probably explained this. I hoped I would never have to sit through a play that Xania directed. And, Samantha Healy could have easily shown up for her class, then slipped out once the play began, and no one would've known. Least of all Xania Divinity.

# CHAPTER EIGHTEEN

Wednesday dawned warm and I decided to get out of the city. I enjoyed a beautiful drive as I headed southwest into the foothills to Cal's house to find out what he'd learned about Samantha Healy.

Cal's home office couldn't be more dissimilar from mine. Where I have books, videos, pictures, and other valuable items, and one computer, Cal has nothing in his office but computers – four to be exact – and other computer-related stuff. To be fair, there is a ratty loveseat to sit on at your own risk, and a chair that Cal wheels from monitor to monitor across the hardwood floors. But it isn't hard to grasp what is important to the man, and it isn't anything aesthetic.

Stacks of books, manuals, and boxes of computer parts cover most of the available floor area, and a plethora of dirty dishes growing science projects were strewn about the long tables where the computers were set up. This was where Cal lived, where he was truly at home. He even watched DVD's on a 30-inch computer monitor. If he could've fit his twin bed in the office, I'm sure he would sleep here, too.

"You checked out Denver Alternative College last night?" Cal asked once we were settled in his office.

"Uh-huh." I sprawled out on the loveseat, ignoring the stale air and dust I created when I upset the cushions. I shaded my eyes against the bright sunlight coming into the room from a small window over the couch.

By the time I finished relating my encounter with Xania Divinity, Cal was on the floor.

"Stop," he gasped, his whole body shaking with laughter. "Man, that's priceless."

"As is Xania. Talk about a legend in her own mind," I chuckled. "I did look up her name online, though. She has some acting credits, mostly some minor television roles in the late '60's and '70's, and some off-Broadway plays, so I guess she knows something about the theater."

"Hoo boy." Cal wiped tears from his eyes, crawled back into his chair, and became serious. "You doubt Samantha's alibi?"

I nodded. "I don't think Xania has the first clue if Samantha stayed the whole time or not. I'll have to interview each student in all the acting classes to find out if Samantha left early or not, and who knows if any of them would remember."

"What'd you find out about Ned's insurance policy?" Cal asked.

I turned on my left side, which eased some of the discomfort from my broken ribs. I was breathing normally but still experienced a bit of pain when I moved in just the right way.

"I called Jack and got the information about the company, and gave them a call." I said. "The agent I talked to wouldn't reveal who it was that called him. He kept saying it was an anonymous person, but he slipped more than once and said 'her' or 'she'."

"Samantha."

"That's what I think," I said. "Ned's policy has been sitting there since his death, but it's at the instigation of the deceased's relatives or the beneficiary to get the ball rolling. In the case of Ned Healy, this anonymous phone call did that. The agent has to receive a death certificate, and then the insurance company will make the claim. A little bit of paperwork, and they release the money to Samantha. I called the county coroner, and it's not that hard to get a death certificate either."

"Huh." Cal twisted up his face, thinking. "Any reasons why the insurance company wouldn't release the money?"

"The usual – suicide. But Ned's death was officially ruled as an accident. It's nice and tidy for Samantha."

"So we have motive."

"Right. Money – one million big ones. And we have the means. Samantha could've left her class and gotten Ned to go with her up into the mountains for a bike ride, and then she pushes him off the trail."

"How would she get home?"

"She either rides back, or she has an accomplice pick her up somewhere, maybe at the trail head, and they drive back to Denver."

"But Ned hated the mountains, right?"

"He hated heights. Jack said that he didn't like cycling, or the mountains. But we only have Jack's word that Ned was afraid of heights. Maybe Ned went to therapy and worked on that. And who better to talk Ned into going up on that trail than his ex-wife?"

Cal mulled that over. "It's possible. I don't like going riding, but you got me to do it."

"Exactly." I stared at the tiny dots in the popcorn ceiling. "I wish I could get into Samantha's house, find out if she has any barbiturates, or if she could easily get her hands on some pills that she could've slipped in Ned's drink or something."

"Sounds like you've been watching too much late-night television."

"Sometimes the means and motive are so obvious you gloss right over them."

"I might be able to shed some light on Samantha's ability to get the drugs," Cal said, grabbing some papers from the table.

"Oh yeah?"

"Samantha Healy," Cal said, propelling his chair next to the couch. "Formerly known as Samantha Simpson. Do you want her vital statistics?"

"Not unless it has a direct bearing on this case."

Something crinkling underneath me, so I reached down between the couch pillows and pulled out a half full bag of potato chips, now mangled to crumbs.

"Lovely," I said, holding the bag up.

Cal tossed the bag into the corner, onto a pile of papers and other stuff I didn't want to imagine.

"You don't want to know her age. Okay." He paused. "Do you want to know that she's thirty?"

"You just told me."

"She's five-foot eight, a hundred and thirty pounds."

"What does this have to do with the price of rice in China?"

"Nothing. It was part of my research." Cal shot me a pious look.

I sat up and rubbed my neck, trying to ward off a headache.

"Okay, I'm focusing. You said you had something about Samantha getting drugs."

"Right." Cal waved a paper in front of my face. "Samantha has a criminal past."

"What?" I snatched the paper from him. "When? What for?"

"Samantha Simpson was busted for possession eight years ago." I did some quick math. "That was four years before she married Ned."

"What'd they find on her?" I asked, scanning the notes. Cal had printed out all the related offenses Samantha had been charged with.

"Samantha was stopped for erratic driving, was combative, and was subsequently taken to jail. When she was searched, lo and behold, she had a number of Seconal pills in her purse."

"Not very bright," I said.

"She was in college," Cal said. We both knew how stupid young people could be – the remembrance of our infamous flour tortilla drug purchase was enough for us to look on Samantha's actions with a certain tempered sympathy.

"The police report said that Samantha claimed she didn't know how the drugs got there, but who would say 'Yes, the drugs are mine' when they're being arrested?"

"And she had enough on her to get charged with possession with intent to sell. Because it was her first offense, she got probation and community service," I said, finishing the report. I gave the paper back to Cal. "Samantha obviously knew how to get her hands on the stuff."

"If she did then, she could now," Cal said.

"And she's familiar with the effects. She would know that Seconal would make Ned drowsy, if not put him to sleep. Easier for her to get him in the car and up into the mountains."

"But how would she get him on a bike?"

"She wouldn't have to drug him that much, just enough to make him a little loopy. Then he's more easily manipulated."

"True."

"And it can't be that hard for her to get her hands on the drugs. I'd bet there's at least a few students in her class that use something."

"She drops a pill or two in a drink she gives Ned, then takes him for a ride, they go around that bend, and he's gone."

"That was my theory," I said.

"I'm coming on board."

"Oh." I reached for the phone. "I'm hungry. Let's get some lunch."

"Yeah, detective work really takes it out of you." Cal shot me a goofy grin.

I ordered us a pepperoni and mushroom pizza, and while we waited for the delivery, we worked on a crossword puzzle. Let me correct – Cal worked on the puzzle, a tough New York Times one, and I mostly watched, adding one answer about Alfred Hitchcock's first sound film – *Blackmail*, made in 1929, in case you wanted to know. We were halfway through when the doorbell clanged.

Cal left to pay the pizza guy, and my cell phone rang.

"Hello, is that you Reed?" Henri Benoit's accent cut in and out like a bad television signal.

"Yes. Henri, I can hardly hear you."

I stood up and moved around the room, trying to get a better connection.

"There is..." The line crackled. "You should..." I tried the hallway.

"Henri, I can't hear you."

The line suddenly cleared, and Henri's breathing blared through the phone. In the background, the bell in his shop chimed.

"Why are you yelling?" Henri asked. "I don't understand this business with the cell phones. You think if you cannot hear someone, it will help if you yell into the phone. I can hear you just fine."

"I can hear you now," I said. I didn't tell him that I was standing on the toilet in Cal's bathroom. Must be the porcelain making a better connection.

"I have to talk to you," Henri continued.

"Okay, shoot."

"No, not over the phone. I want to show you something."

"About the poster?" A burst of excitement sizzled through me and I dropped the phone. It hit the tile floor with a clunk. Henri's disembodied voice crackled up at me.

"Henri, wait Henri. I can't hear you." I shouted again as I snatch up the phone. Now the connection was really bad.

"What do you think of that?"

"What? I dropped the phone, Henri. I didn't hear what you said."

The phone buzzed and hummed at me. "Why...wait...come down...until six."

"I'll come down to the shop," I interpreted the sounds.

"Ah, yes...stop shouting...can't be possible."

The line went dead.

"Damn it," I said, then used the tried and true way of fixing any gadget that was giving me a problem. I banged the phone on the counter top, then put it to my ear. Nothing.

"That'll solve the problem," Cal said from the doorway. He had the pizza box in one hand, some papers towels in the other, and an amused look on his face.

"It's worked before," I mumbled as I followed him back into the office. It didn't matter. Now I had an excuse to go back to Henri's shop and marvel at all the collectibles.

# CHAPTER NINETEEN

After our late lunch and some time playing computer games, I left Cal's house and drove down the twisting dirt road to Highway 285.

I cranked the air conditioner, turned left, and headed back toward Denver. It was four o'clock, but I was moving against the flow of commuters heading home to the mountains, and even with the endless construction traffic on 285, I had plenty of time to get to Henri's shop before it closed. A gang of construction workers sweated under the intense heat of the sun, and I was thankful that I was sitting in the 4-Runner with cool air blasting on me. I didn't envy them a bit.

I pulled into a space on Broadway a little before 5:00, locked the car, and strolled to Henri's shop. The chimes above the door announced my entry into Classic Hollywood Memorabilia, and a wave of cool air hit me as I shut the door. I took off my sunglasses and looked around, but didn't see Henri or anyone else.

"Hello?" I called out, thinking I heard a door at the back of the shop close. Henri sometimes exited through a rear exit to the alley where he parked his car and where the trash dumpsters were located. Since it was the end of the day, maybe he was taking the trash out.

I called his name again, louder this time.

Nothing.

I meandered around a locked display case full of autographed pictures, letting my eyes linger on the various items as I made my way to the back counter. Among the objects were a number of Charlie Chaplin pieces. There was an autographed picture of Charlie Chaplin in his tramp garb. I remembered reading in a collector's book that photos of The Tramp signed by Chaplin were rare. This one was in pristine condition, with a price of $12,000, a bargain for a Chaplin collector. Next to it was Chaplin's book, My Trip Abroad, written in 1921. I wondered how Henri acquired such a rare find. I didn't see a price tag on it, but a signed picture of Edna Purviance, Chaplin's leading lady in many of his early silent films, had a price of $300. I lingered for a moment, wondering about the actors and their lives. What was going on in Charlie's life when he signed the photo? Why did Edna Purviance's career falter after she quit working with Chaplin? Okay, I'm weird like that.

I glanced up from the display case. "Henri?" I called again.

I studied a couple of posters on the wall before I moved over to the counter. Sean Connery stared down at me, the dashing secret agent holding the Walter PPK up near his face. Next to that were nice copies of the first two James Bond movies, *Dr. No* and *Goldfinger*. I could only hope my Bogart poster would look as good as the ones Henri had hanging on the walls. I leaned my elbows on the counter and waited for Henri to return.

After a moment, I pushed aside a stack of papers, bored. Some of the bold lettering in Henri's sloping handwriting on the top paper caught my attention: "Academy Award".

"Interesting," I said to no one as I turned the page so I could read it better.

Henri had written a list and jotted notes beside some of the points:

Statuette weight: 6 ¾ lbs

Height: 13 1/2"

Plaster molding


"A little bit of research?" I again talked as if Henri were in the room listening to me. "Statuette base: solid black marble." I continued to read: "The statue sits on a canister of film, with 8 cutouts in the reel."

Little bits of trivia I didn't know, but it made for captivating reading, at least if you had any curiosity about the Academy Awards. I did know that the Academy Award was officially named the Academy Award of Merit, that it was nicknamed "Oscar" but the origins of the nickname are under some dispute, and that the number of awards and categories have been in flux since the Academy first started giving out the awards at a banquet in 1929. And I knew that an Oscar was worth over $10,000 brand new.

I read on, pausing occasionally to decipher Henri's writing. I was thoroughly engrossed in Henri's notes when I heard a car starting up outside. I stopped reading, cocked my head like a dog, and listened.

After a moment, I heard the noise again, and this time it sounded distinctly human.

"Henri?" I said loudly, my eyes roving around the store.

I heard the noise a third time, and it sounded like a groan.

"Is that you?" I stepped around the counter and poked my head into the back room. Nothing but a wood table, and an organizer box containing scissors, knives, other tools, and pens.

And Henri Benoit lying in a crumpled mess on the floor, his legs tucked underneath him at an awkward angle, his bifocals broken on the floor near him. A pool of blood had formed underneath his head. In a cursory glance I couldn't see where he was wounded, but his white ponytail was turning a dark shade of crimson.

"Henri!" I shouted, dropping on my knees beside him. I gently touched his shoulder and looked into his eyes. They had a glassy sheen to them.

"Oh no!" My hands shook as I placed a finger to his neck. A faint pulse beat against my skin. Henri was alive, but just barely.

I had to try three times before I could get my cell phone out of my pocket, and I chided myself to calm down as I dialed 911. The operator spoke in a gravelly voice as she took down the address. She said she was sending an ambulance, and told me not to touch Henri. She tried to keep me on the phone, but I hung up.

"What happened?" I asked Henri.

His near lifeless form didn't move, but his eyelids flickered, reminding me, strangely enough, of an old movie reel in slow motion. I watched his chest. It rose a millimeter, then sank again. Over and over.

"Come on, Henri. Hang on." I sat back on my haunches, feeling totally helpless, and waited.

Finally, faint sounds of sirens permeated the silence.

"They're coming," I murmured to Henri. His face was pale, and it seemed that his breathing grew even shallower.

The sirens' blare grew louder, and then the floor vibrated as trucks rumbled slowly to a stop out on Broadway. I left Henri and ran out to the front of the store.

"He's in here!" I bellowed, frantically waving my arms toward the store entrance. As the rescue workers hopped out of the ambulance, a police car screeched to a stop in front of the fire truck.

I guided two firemen, a trio of paramedics, and two police officers to the back of the store. Two paramedics rolled a stretcher covered with white sheets between them. On it they had piled a couple of boxes of supplies. They hurried around the display cases to the back room, leaving the stretcher by the counter.

"Step back here, sir," said one of the firemen, an ox of a man with thick arms and a large square jaw, as he pushed me back.

"What happened to him?" one of the paramedics asked me.

"I don't know. I came in and heard him back here."

I stood just outside the door and watched as the paramedics set to work on Henri. One put a pressure cuff on his arm, and another carefully lifted one of Henri's eyelids, shining a flashlight in his eyes.

"Do you know him?" The third one, a woman, glanced up at me as she prepared an oxygen mask to put over Henri's nose and mouth. The other two talked to each other in clipped tones.

I nodded mutely.

"Do you know his health history? Is he allergic to any medications?"

"No," I said, my voice faltering. "I don't know." I knew very little of that kind of information.

"Do you know what happened here?" one of the officers asked me, oblivious to the conversation I'd just had. I had to look up to answer because he was so tall and thin.

"No," I muttered, my attention riveted to Henri and the rescue work.

I was vaguely aware of the officer talking to his partner while I watched the paramedics. After a minute of hurried but efficient work, the woman spoke into a small, square mike attached to her shoulder. She waited for a response before placing a towel under Henri's head. She barked a couple of orders, and the other two assembled a makeshift carrier underneath Henri.

"Is he going to be okay?" I asked.

One paramedic, so young I wondered if he was still in high school, turned to me as they lifted Henri with the makeshift gurney and settled him onto the stretcher.

Instead of answering my question, the paramedic said, "What's his name?"

"Henri Benoit."

"Are you a family member? His son?" the female paramedic asked. Her bright red hair belied her calm, bedside tone.

"No. I'm a friend," I said. "Is he going to be all right?" I asked again.

"At the very least he's sustained a head injury. We won't know the extent until we can get him to the hospital for tests." The woman held back as the other two paramedics started rolling the stretcher out of the store. "We're taking him to St. Anthony's Central," she said as she followed them. "You know where that is?"

"Yes," I said as I followed them, keeping vigil until Henri was safely installed in the back of the rescue vehicle. The fire truck and rescue vehicles blocked one lane of traffic, and people gawked as they slowly drove past.

The engine started up, and the rear doors of the ambulance slammed shut. I stared into the back window. Henri lay with the oxygen mask over his face. The paramedics continued to attend to him as the truck pulled away, engine grumbling and sirens wailing. The fire truck took off, and I stood in the street until the hoses and ladder disappeared from view.

"I'm Officer Hammer," the tall one said as he pulled me back to the sidewalk.

"Officer Grossman," the second officer said to me. "We'd like to ask you a few questions." He was in his late forties, with chubby cheeks and a spare tire around his waist. Tufts of gray hair fell in a mish-mash way as he scratched his head. He held out a meaty hand, indicating that I should accompany him back to the shop.

"Did you know him?"

"Yes," I said, coming out of my shock. I gave him as much detail as I could about Henri.

"What happened?"

I launched into an explanation as Officer Hammer came in. While Officer Grossman and I talked, he tramped to the back of the store.

"Henri was expecting me," I said. "We were going to talk about a poster he was appraising. When I came in, I thought the shop was empty, so I waited. After a few minutes, I heard Henri. I found him on the floor like that, and called for help."

"Where did you think he was?"

"Outside in back. That's where he parks."

If the explanation satisfied Officer Grossman, he didn't show it. He jotted down my answers in a tiny notebook.

"Place is clean," Hammer said. "No sign of forced entry, no sign of a weapon, and the cash box under the counter's got a wad of cash and a few checks in it."

"They could've taken some memorabilia," I said.

Hammer shrugged. "We won't know that until the victim..." he paused and cleared his throat, "until Mister Ben..." he stumbled over the name, "until your friend can do a thorough inventory."

"Do you have any information about his family?" Roberts asked me.

"His wife's name is Evaline."

"We'll need to get in touch with her," Hammer said.

"I'll call her," I said. "It'll be much easier to hear this from me."

"Do you know Mr. Benoit that well?" Roberts continued. He pronounced the name perfectly and received a glare from Hammer for his efforts.

"We're friends," I said, stretching the truth.

"Okay," Roberts hesitated, but both he and Hammer looked relieved. Better for me to deliver the news about Henri than them.

"Can you lock up here?" This from Roberts.

"Sure. I'll take care of everything."

"We'll wait." Roberts took a relaxed stance and crossed his arms. They obviously weren't going to leave me here alone. I couldn't blame them. Hammer asked for my personal information, and didn't seem impressed when I handed him my business card.

"Doing a little snooping?" Hammer tucked my card in his pocket.

"I was here on business," I said.

"How about an ID?" Hammer asked.

I dug out my wallet and handed him my license. He wrote down everything and handed it back. "You'll stay in town, right?" He said as if he were speaking to an imbecile.

"Of course." I was getting irritated, knowing full well they thought of me as a suspect.

They spent a few more minutes in the back of the shop while I tried to find Henri's home phone number, but I could feel Hammer's eyes on me as I went to the counter and found a Rolodex. Silently thanking Henri for holding on to some old-fashioned ways, I spun the wheel until I found the "B's", and in seconds I was dialing Henri's phone.

"Allo?" a light and airy voice asked.

"Mrs. Benoit?"

"Yes?"

I identified myself. Although I had never met Henri's wife, she obviously knew who I was, because she immediately began discussing how much Henri liked talking old movies with me. I had to interrupt her to tell her about Henri.

"My Henri! Is he okay?" Her accent was not as thick as Henri's, but her fear and concern sizzled through the phone lines.

I explained what I knew and told her where the paramedics had taken Henri. I said that I would close the shop and meet her there as soon as I could, and hung up.

For the first time since I found Henri, I let my nerves settle. I sucked in a deep breath and let it out slowly. Focus, I thought to myself.

I tiptoed into the back office, watching the officers. Hammer was speaking into a radio, probably getting a background check on me, and Roberts was examining the back door.

I stood near the spot where Henri had fallen and let my eyes wander around the room. I didn't see anything out of place, at least from what I remembered of the room. I didn't see my poster, but Henri could've had it stored somewhere, awaiting my arrival. The pens and paper that he kept on a shelf above the table appeared undisturbed. The trashcan on the floor was tipped over and a few crumpled papers were strewn out, but nothing else seemed wrong.

Except for the spot of blood soaking into the carpet. I shook my head in dismay. Who would do such a thing to someone like Henri? A robber?

I eased out of the office and made my way through the rest of the store, but I didn't see anything missing from the display cases. But there were so many items. How could I know if something was stolen?

I felt helpless, and hoped Henri would be all right.

# CHAPTER TWENTY

"Time to go, buddy." Hammer emerged from the office. "Let's lock this place up."

"I don't have a set of keys," I said. "For the deadbolt," I explained.

Roberts poked his head out. "Do the best you can."

I pulled down the shades in the front windows and on the door, flipped the sign hanging in the window from "Open" to "Closed", and locked the doorknob. I then went to the back, where a series of switches controlled the lighting throughout the shop. I flipped them off, watching the room grow dark from front to back.

Since Henri's burglar alarm system was easy to activate, I turned it on, Hammer watching my every move. I had to hope that Evaline would know the code if someone had to get in before Henri became conscious, but Henri had way too many valuable things in the store that needed to be protected.

"That's it," I said. Hammer and Roberts waited for me to exit, then followed me out the door.

The beeping of the alarm signaled, and I let myself out the back door and walked around the building to my car. The officers waited until I pulled out into traffic before they returned to their car. I needed to find out what happened here, if for no other reason than to clear my own name.

» » » » »

A friend of mine was brought in a while ago," I said to the emergency room nurse at St. Anthony's Central a half hour later. "His name is Henri Benoit."

"Oh, are you Reed Ferguson?" an accented voice behind me said.

I turned and gazed into the tear-filled mocha eyes of Evaline Benoit. She was a petite woman not much taller than five feet. Her long silvery hair was pulled into a bun with an expensive mother-of-pearl hairpiece holding it in place, and dangling from her ears were round blue earrings that matched her dress.

"Yes." I bent down and Evaline rose up on her toes to plant a light kiss on both my cheeks in European fashion.

"They don't tell me anything about my Henri," she said, holding a small white handkerchief to her lips, muffling a sob.

I murmured assurances while she wept into the hanky, then guided her to a couch in the waiting area. After a few moments she composed herself, drying her eyes and blowing her nose.

"They say that Henri must have tests. They need to see what has happened to his head."

"Someone hit him on the back of the head," I said. She nodded, the hanky halfway to her face.

"Were there any other injuries?"

"They do not think so. But they don't tell me." Her body shook.

"Let me see what I can find out."

She thanked me profusely. I went to the desk and spoke briefly with the nurse.

"They're completing tests right now," I said when I returned. I sat down next to Evaline. "We should know something soon."

"You are such a nice boy," Evaline said. I tried not to blush. "Henri, he likes you very much, and I can see why."

I thanked her, but she was already lost in her concerns, staring with unseeing eyes at the wall. We waited in silence until a doctor came out to tell us that Henri was in the ICU.

"Your husband has sustained a head injury. X-rays showed a hairline fracture above the left temporal lobe, and right now he's in a coma. We won't know the extent of brain damage, if any, until he wakes up."

Tears rolled down Evaline's cheeks. "Brain damage?"

"We don't know anything yet," the doctor stressed. "He may be just fine. We'll be monitoring him, but right now all we can do is wait."

"Can I see him?" Evaline asked.

"Certainly."

We stood up as the doctor left to talk to the admitting nurse.

"I'll leave you with Henri," I said. "I'll come by here tomorrow to check on you."

"Thank you." Evaline stretched out an arm and patted my face.

"Is there anything I can do to help?"

She shook her head. "No. I have called our daughter. She lives in New York, but she will come out now."

"Good," I said. The doctor escorted her to an intensive care area, and then I left.

» » » » »

Halfway home my cell phone rang.

"I've been trying to reach you all day," Jack Healy said when I answered. "Do you ever go to your office?"

"I've had a busy day," I said, not wanting to explain the events of the last few hours. It was after nine, but weariness was setting in, and it felt like the middle of the night.

"Have you found out anything more?"

"I checked on Samantha's alibi. I doubt it would stand up in court."

"She could've killed Ned," Jack said, an edge in his voice.

"It's possible. Or she could've set him up. But I don't have any proof of that." I kept my answers short. With everything that had happened to Henri, I wasn't prepared to give him an update just yet. But I had to admit that Samantha made a likely candidate. And I couldn't brush aside a feeling that I'd missed some piece of information, something that didn't set right.

"What more do you need?"

"More than I've got, Jack. This is all speculation. You can't charge her with a crime if you don't have proof."

"It's not like she's going to come out and tell you she killed Ned," he snorted.

"Look, I'm running down a few things now," I said. "Give me a few more days, and I'll be able to give you a point-by-point account."

"You're making progress?"

"Yes," I hedged a bit. I was making progress, but wasn't sure in what direction just yet.

"Fine."

Jack didn't sound fine, but what else could he say? He was smart enough to know I was right, but desperate enough to want to hang Ned's death on the first likely candidate. Not a good combination.

The moon shone brightly in the night sky as I pulled into my alley garage. I walked through the backyard to the front porch, where metal stairs led up to my condo.

I checked the mailbox by the Goofball Brothers' door and was starting upstairs when I heard their door open.

"Dude, how's it going?" Deuce came out on the porch, wearing nothing but a pair of cut-off jeans. "We're going to go play some pool. You want to come?"

"I'm tired and it's late," I said. "But thanks."

"It's only nine-thirty." Deuce looked at an imaginary watch on his wrist. "It's not that late."

"Thanks, but I've had a long day. You might want to get dressed first." I smiled at him.

"Yeah, I will." Deuce stared at me for a second. "Are you okay?" He took a step closer to me, squinting. Then his eyes widened in surprise.

"Hey, man. You're hurt!" He pointed at my side.

I gazed down and saw a spot on my shirt. I hadn't noticed it before. I tugged at the fabric, examining the reddish-brown stain, and with a sudden pang of sadness, realized it was Henri's blood. I had no idea how it got there. I didn't remember touching him, or the pool of blood on the carpet, but I must've.

"I'm fine," I reassured Deuce. "A friend of mine was hurt today."

"Is he all right?"

"I'm not sure."

Ace came out onto the porch, holding an empty glass. "Who's fine?" he asked, wiping a milk mustache off his face.

"He is," Deuce said, jabbing a finger at me. "But his friend's not."

"Not what?"

"Fine."

"Okay, don't tell me," Ace said, punching Deuce on the arm.

"Hey, why'd you do that?"

"Because you didn't answer me."

"I did too!"

"Fine."

"Fine who?"

"What?"

With a shake of my head, I left the brothers to their impromptu spin-off of "Who's On First," and wearily climbed the stairs to my condo, where I showered and tumbled into a dark and restless sleep.

# CHAPTER TWENTY-ONE

Denver Alternative College is a lot busier during the day than it is in the evening. I found this out when I walked through the main entrance to the school around lunchtime on Thursday and had to dodge a moving mass of people on my way to a food court.

After a brief visit to the hospital to check on Henri, I made some phone calls to the DAC registrar's office. With some slick bending of the truth, I got a list of students that were enrolled in Samantha's acting class. The youthful-sounding man in the enrollment office was more than happy to provide the information when I said I was a producer for a major Hollywood firm, and we were looking for prospects for a new movie that would be filming in Denver in the fall.

A number of Samantha's fellow students in the "Actors and Acting" class were also enrolled in a course at one o'clock, entitled "The Essence of Acting," taught by the inimitable Xania Divinity. These students might be able to tell me something about Samantha's character. I hoped that some of them might know if she was a drug user, and what her relationship with Ned was like. And, if any student remembered seeing Samantha leave class before the student play finished, I'd have something to confront her with.

The first person on the class list was Erin Abel. I contacted her, and with more twisting of the truth, I explained to her that I was interested in meeting actors for a potential part in a movie. She took the bait, and we arranged to meet in the student lounge. I told her that I'd probably be the only person in the cafeteria wearing a Colorado Rockies baseball cap over a bad haircut.

Erin Abel had agreed to meet me for a few minutes before her class, so I sat in a crowded lounge at a corner table and waited.

At exactly 12:45, a brunette who couldn't have been of legal drinking age came up to the table.

"Are you Archie Goodwin?" she asked, letting a backpack fall from her shoulder onto the table.

I nodded. Erin apparently had never read Rex Stout mysteries and didn't recognize the name of super-heavy, super-sleuth Nero Wolfe's famous sidekick.

Erin apparently didn't get the memo that it was close to a hundred degrees outside, either. She wore black jeans, a black blouse, and black heels. Her eyes were rimmed with heavy black liner, and her complexion was so pale I knew she had to be using powder on her face, but to give some color to her ensemble, she had silver bracelets and earrings.

*Modeling an elegant Goth look, we have Erin Abel*, I thought.

"Erin?" I stood up and shook her cold and clammy hand. Not what I expected in this heat.

"You weren't kidding about the haircut," she said.

"Car accident," I replied, lifting my cap to let her see the stitches.

"Ouch." Erin plopped into a plastic chair across from me. "So you're looking for actors for your next movie?" She pulled out a package of cigarettes and started to light one, then stopped abruptly. "Damn. I keep forgetting we can't smoke in here."

I suppressed a smile.

"What kind of work have you done?" I asked. I couldn't just blurt out questions about Samantha; I would have to play it a little cagier.

"I've done some local theater, and I was in some of my high school plays." Erin listed her credits with a starving actor's enthusiasm. My guilt grew as she spouted off her range of abilities, even speaking in a number of credible accents.

"You're quite good," I said. "We may have a small part for you, especially if you can work on your Scottish accent."

Erin's face lit up. I should've gone to jail for buttering her up like I did, but I needed information. And if I said I was a detective, I probably wouldn't get any. Not only that, Samantha would learn that I was asking about her.

"This would be in the fall?" Erin asked. She stuffed the unused cigarette back in the package.

I nodded. "Would you be willing to change your appearance for the role?"

"Uh-huh. This is no big deal, really," she said, toying with an earring as she talked. "I played a punk rocker in a play and sort of kept the look. But I'll do what I need to for the part."

"You'll probably have to submit to a drug test. For insurance purposes."

"I'm clean." Erin frowned as if I had offended her.

"Just part of the process," I said. I tapped my fingers on the table and tried to look pensive. "I need another actor, a woman. Someone tall and thin, maybe five-eight or so, with blond hair."

"You just described half the women in the school."

"Yes, but I believe I saw someone here before. Sandra, Sally. With a last name like Hedley, or Henry. Something like that."

"Samantha Healy?"

I snapped my fingers. "That's it. I saw Samantha in the student audition play last month. She was quite good."

"She wasn't in the play."

Oops.

"Are you sure? I know I've heard that name somewhere. She's tall and blond, with brown eyes and a big smile. I remember the smile." I hoped I wasn't overdoing it.

"Yeah, that's her."

"If she wasn't in the play, maybe I saw her in the crowd."

"Maybe."

"Was she there?"

Erin scowled. "Yeah, she was there, but I think she left early."

"Are you sure?" I feigned disinterest, but my nerves surged with excitement.

"The play was so bad, a lot of people left," she said with a disgusted grunt. "They didn't cast the better actors."

"Like you."

"Yeah, like me." There wasn't a hint of arrogance in her tone, just a cool assurance.

"Do you know Samantha?"

"Uh-huh."

"Would she be interested in a role in the movie?"

"You're looking to fill more than one role," she said flatly, like she didn't believe I had a part for her.

"Of course. I've got a lot of roles to fill, and I'm looking for new talent. There are plenty of parts to go around, for you, and for Samantha.

If she fits the role right, and she passes the drug test. Just like you."

She chewed at the side of her cheek.

"What?"

"I've got a friend, Carrie Lutz. She has the physical build you're looking for, and she might fit the role better."

"Hmm. Maybe, but Samantha did catch my eye."

Erin leaned on the table. "Look, mister. I don't want to ruin her chances, but Samantha might not be your best bet."

"Why do you say that?"

"She's not a very good actor, and she's hard to work with. She doesn't remember her lines well, and she's seems spacey sometimes. And she dropped her purse one time, and prescriptions bottles fell out. She's not stable, if you know what I mean."

I played the part of disappointed movie producer, but I really wanted to question her more.

"Hey, I have to go to class now, but you really should meet my friend Carrie. She's what you're looking for." Hence the slandering of Samantha Healy.

"I'll think about that," I said. We strolled out of the student lounge, and I said I would be in contact with the school in the fall. The words tasted like garbage as I said them. It was probably the puppy-dog desperation in the kid's eyes that did it.

» » » » »

I left the school with a ravenous appetite. As I walked to the parking lot, the heat of the day created translucent waves that shimmered off the hot pavement. I donned sunglasses to ward off the glare of the sunlight, and was about to get in my car when I heard a shout behind me.

"You asshole!"

Erin Abel came running up to me, her eyes fiery, tears streaming down her cheeks.

"What?" I said.

"You're not a movie producer!"

"Of course I am."

"You are not!" Erin was pissed. "Xania saw us leave and she asked me why I was talking to you. She told me you're a detective. That's why you were asking all those questions."

"It's not what you think," I said.

"Really?"

I floundered around, but couldn't keep up the lie. I finally hung my head. "Erin, I'm sorry. I didn't think you'd talk to me if you knew who I was."

"That was a shitty thing to do." Her dark makeup ran down her face. "Do you know how hard it is to find work? Especially when you're judged so much by the way you look?"

I wanted to tell her that if she was worried about her appearance not being right she was in the wrong profession, but I kept my jaw locked.

"I want to work in the movies. I don't care doing what. I'm just following a dream. But you could care less."

"That's not true." I could relate to following dreams more than she'd know.

"Don't bother coming around here. I'll make sure everyone knows you're after Samantha," she spat at me.

"I wouldn't tell her I was asking around," I said. It sounded lame as I said it.

"Yeah, try to stop me."

Erin stepped back and crossed her arms, acting tough. "Does she think you're an asshole, too?"

Probably, I thought as I got into the 4-Runner and drove away.

» » » » »

My appetite had not-so-mysteriously disappeared, so I put my guilt and shame into a hard workout at the gym. Unfortunately, it didn't help. I was a nice guy. Or I was supposed to be. I didn't like myself at that moment.

I had told Evaline I would check Henri's store so she could stay at the hospital, so that was my next stop. Fortunately, everything was still closed up and the place appeared just as I had left it.

I drove to the hospital with my mind still on Erin Abel. Poor kid, I thought. It's difficult to be young and trying to find your niche in the world, but it's worse when someone takes advantage of you. I'd have to see if I could work out a mea culpa with her. If she'd even talk to me again.

I arrived to the hospital just as a front of ominous clouds darkened the skies. A brisk wind swirled around me as I hurried inside to the intensive care unit. Evaline was there, keeping vigil over Henri.

"How's he doing?" I whispered, taking a seat next to her. She was leaning an arm on the bed, holding Henri's hand.

"He sleeps and mumbles. Sometimes he wakes and looks at me. But the doctors say this is a good sign." Evaline stroked his hand affectionately. "He will be all right, my Henri. You wait and see."

We sat in companionable silence for a bit, listening to the beeps of heart monitors, the occasional cough from other patients, and conversations in hushed tones. I fought against a sense of doom. Hospitals did that to me. The sickness, the decay, all masked in an antiseptic, artificially clean smell that was even worse here in the ICU.

I watched Henri. He seemed to be breathing okay, and his face was peaceful.

"Would you stay with my Henri for a while?" Evaline asked after a bit. "I need to use the ladies' room."

"Sure," I said, scooting my chair closer to the bed.

Evaline stood up and leaned over the bed. She gently straightened Henri's hair and pecked him on the cheek.

I watched her tiptoe away. I sat back in the chair and was fighting drowsiness when Henri began mumbling.

"Henri, you're okay," I said, trying to come up with soothing words and phrases.

His eyes flickered open.

"Henri, it's me. Reed." I smiled at him, but wished Evaline would come back. She needed to talk to him more than I.

"He had it," Henri murmured, his eyes focusing somewhere over my head. "He…"

"What? Who had what?" I glanced over my shoulder, but no one was there.

Henri rolled his head from side to side.

"You have it." His eyes closed.

"Have what?" I whispered. I didn't know if Henri even realized I was there, I just figured it was good to get him talking.

"Your poster." Henri startled me. He was staring right at me, eyes wide open.

"Yes, you have my poster. Is it a valuable poster?"

"The poster. He checked…" Henri heaved a sigh.

I waited.

"His stuff," Henri mumbled.

I patted his arm. "Okay, Henri. It's okay."

Henri smiled at me, then drifted off. Since Henri and I were supposed to meet when he was attacked, I wondered if seeing my face was triggering his memory.

Evaline came back, interrupting my thoughts.

"How is he?"

"He seemed to be talking to me a second ago, but now he's asleep."

Evaline sat down and took up her position of holding his hand. "He sees you. That is good. If he doesn't know what he is saying, that is okay."

"I need to go, but I'll come by again tomorrow." I stood up.

Evaline touched my arm. "Thank you. You're such a nice boy."

Huh. I wondered what Erin Abel would say about that.

I nodded and left.

# CHAPTER TWENTY-TWO

Do you ever have one of those days where you wish you could hit a rewind button and start over? Not only had I bungled my detective work, making myself look like Inspector Clouseau instead of Nero Wolfe, but I had lied to and offended a young woman who had done nothing to me, and ruined any chance of talking to Samantha's fellow actors. I also likely put Samantha onto my trail, turning the tables on myself. And to top it off, Henri was in the hospital.

I wanted to crawl into a cave and hibernate.

I holed up in my condo instead. A thunderous storm had drenched the city, then quickly rolled eastward, leaving a pleasant touch of moisture in the cool evening air but it didn't refresh me. I changed from my pseudo-Hollywood producer slacks and dress shirt to a T-shirt and shorts. I grabbed a beer and sat watching reruns of *Gilligan's Island*. After three episodes, I wondered what so many other astute people have wondered over the years: If the Professor could make a radio out of a coconut, why couldn't he fix a hole in the boat and get them off the island?

I flipped through the channels until I found a classic film noir, *Sweet Smell of Success*, considered by many to be the best film noir movie ever. It played in the background while I grabbed some chips, salsa, and another beer.

*Sweet Smell of Success* switched to *Mildred Pierce*, with Joan Crawford. Another classic film, but I wasn't in the mood for Joan's onscreen tragedies. I searched around but couldn't find the remote. But I did see the note Deuce had written me the night they brought me home from the hospital. It was still attached to the notepad.

I smiled as I reread it. That was a few days ago. Now, the cut on my head itched like a bad sunburn. But the stitches were about to come out, and my ribs were feeling slightly better, so I thought I might as well sever all reminders of that ghastly night. I tore the page off the notepad, crumpled it, and tossed it on the coffee table.

On the next page of the pad were more scribbled notes. I didn't recognize the handwriting at first, but as I read a bit, I realized that this was the notepad I'd taken from Ned's house and this must be Ned's writing. I flipped through the pages until I came to my own notes concerning Ned's real estate transactions.

On the top of that sheet was a handwritten list of websites. Hmm, I hadn't noticed seeing them before. They all seemed related to movies. With a curiosity born of frustration with my lack of progress, I went into my home office and booted up the computer. After a few clicks, I was on the Internet. I typed in the address of the first website on the list.

A colorful page sprung up, displaying all kinds of information about films of the 1940's. I read with enthusiasm, clicking from page to page, and actor to actor. Once I'd exhausted the information from the website, I typed in another address, and this time, the website was all about movie posters.

Humphrey Bogart movies were among the listed items, and I found *The Maltese Falcon* poster that Ned had owned and that was now at Henri's store. It was among four styles originally printed and was thought to be fairly rare.

Ned had obviously been doing some research and must have found a copy of the poster this way. I wondered how much he'd had to pay for it.

I visited a few more websites that were listed on the notepad, reading more on classic movies and old posters. A couple of sites dedicated to Oscar trivia caught my eye as well. I took the quizzes and did fairly well. Too bad having a brain full of Hollywood trivia didn't pay the bills.

The movie on television ended, and I glanced at the computer clock. It was almost midnight. I had completely lost track of the time.

I shut down the computer and tumbled into bed, hoping that tomorrow I could salvage the pieces of my investigation.

» » » » »

I was in the shower the next morning, fantasizing that I'd won the Best Actor Oscar for my performance as The Great Detective, and in the middle of thanking everyone from Humphrey Bogart's spirit to my non-existent agent, it hit me. I'd missed it last night when I was on the computer, but I was almost positive about it now.

I hopped out of the shower, wrapped a towel around my waist, and hurried to the phone, dripping water all over the carpet as I went.

I dialed Henri's cell phone and hoped that Evaline would pick up. I chided myself for forgetting Henri's notes when I left his shop. After four rings, I was sent to voice mail.

"Damn it!" I tossed the phone down and threw on a pair of jeans and a shirt.

I didn't bother with breakfast, but flew out the door, down the stairs and to the garage. In fifteen minutes, I was sprinting into the ICU, where Evaline was perched by Henri's bed, a Bible in her hands. She was quietly reading from the Psalms.

"It keeps him calm," she said, looking up from the book. "It keeps me calm, too."

I pulled up a chair beside her and surveyed Henri. He didn't seem as pale, but he'd taken on a grizzled look with his stubbly jaw and matted hair. He did seem peaceful however, with his chest rising and falling in a steady rhythm.

"Evaline, I need to get into the store," I said. "Henri has something there that I need. I think he was going to give it to me the other day, but by the time I showed up at the shop, he'd already been attacked."

Evaline closed the Bible and swiveled in the chair so she was facing me directly. "But I cannot leave my Henri. What if he wakes up? He will need me."

I reached out and grasped her hand. "I know. That's very important, and I wouldn't be asking if this weren't important as well. It won't take very long."

She searched my eyes. "Okay. If it means that much to you, we will go to the shop."

"Thank you," I murmured.

Evaline gathered up a purse the size of a grocery sack, laid the Bible on a small nightstand by the bed, and followed me to my car. I drove us from St. Anthony's to the shop and parked around back by the alley entrance.

"I set the alarm," I said. "Do you know the code?"

"I think so," Evaline nodded as we walked to the back door.

I hoped she did know the code because I didn't want to see any police at the store again.

"Let me find the right key," Evaline paused by the back door. She dug around in her purse. I thought she'd be able to find Texas in that bag by the time she extracted a set of keys. She fanned them out, and finally selected one.

"Here it is," she said as she inserted it into the lock.

The door opened with a squeak and we stepped through a tiny hallway and into the back workroom area. The room was hot and stuffy, and I immediately began to sweat. Loud beeps pierced the silence. Evaline rushed to the alarm, pressed a few buttons, and the beeping stopped.

"Oh, my Henri loves this place," she mused, her eyes brimming with tears.

I hadn't been aware of the toll this was taking on her. Her eyes seemed more concave, and weary lines etched the soft skin on her face.

"Everything will be fine." I put my arm around her shoulder, trying to comfort her.

After a small moment of tears, Evaline pulled a handkerchief from her purse – she found this right away – dabbed her eyes, and pushed me into the store.

"I'm fine. Go. Find what you need."

I rushed to the counter and found Henri's notes. I perused them quickly and found exactly what I thought I would find: Information about the Oscar statuette, its weight, the reel of film with 8 slots, and details about an award for Luise Rainer. Best Supporting Actress, 1937. The very same description for the same Oscar had been in Ned's scribbled notes.

"Bingo," I said, grabbing the notes.

"Just that?" Evaline came around behind me. "Take them."

"Are you sure?"

She nodded her head vigorously. "It will be fine. You can return it when Henri is better."

"Thank you." I leaned down and planted a kiss on her cheek. She blushed as shyly as a teenager.

"Let's lock up," she said. "I must get back to my Henri."

» » » » »

I drove Evaline back to the hospital and sat with her for a while, but my mind was on the folder that sat on the back seat of the 4-Runner. I was sure I was onto something, but a piece or two were missing.

When it seemed like a polite amount of time had passed, I thanked Evaline for her time, and left.

I nearly ran to the car, jumped in, and defied all traffic laws for speeding as I raced home. I parked on the street and ran up the front porch steps just as Deuce came out of his condo.

"Hey, where's the fire?" he asked. He had on slacks and a nice shirt, a sure sign that he was on his way to work.

"What?" I asked him.

"That's what Bob says whenever I'm in a hurry."

"Oh, yeah." I chuckled. "I finally got a break on the case. That's what I'm going to check on."

"Cool." Deuce pulled the hood of his coat over his head. "It's gray out here."

I was headed up the stairs, but I stopped with one foot in midair.

"What?"

"It's gray." Deuce pointed at the sky, which had turned overcast in the last hour. "It might rain."

"Yeah, it might."

I waved goodbye and continued up the stairs to my place.

I let myself in, grabbed a soda from the refrigerator, and plopped down at the kitchen table. I spread out Henri's notes and read through them carefully. When I was finished, one more brick in the proverbial wall of this case was in place.

Elbows on the table, I stared out the small, square kitchen window that overlooked the backyard. If what I was thinking was true, another question remained. How had Ned gotten the poster?

It all seemed too crazy to be believed.

Menacing clouds formed in the sky. They rolled around, as if they were mulling over the decision whether to rain or not. A bolt of lightning flashed in the distance. The wind was picking up and the branches on the big oak trees in the yard were swaying.

Deuce was right. It was definitely gray out.

I sat up.

Some tidbit of a clue hovered around in my brain, just out of grasp of my conscious retrieval. It was right there, so close I could almost touch it. What had I missed?

I went to the living room and again looked at the notepad that I'd taken from Ned's house. I flipped through his notes until I found it.

A list of colors. Including "gray", with a circle around it.

I grabbed Ned's real estate files and my notes. The connection hit me like a bullet. I rushed into the other room, searched the Internet for a number, picked up the phone and dialed.

"Edna? It's..." I paused. "Philip Marlowe," I said, hoping that was the same name I'd used when I'd met her in Conifer. When she didn't react, I said, "I met you at your place and we talked about your father's house."

"Oh, yes. You're the young man who was interested in architecture. How are you?"

"I'm fine, thanks. I was doing some research about the neighborhood around 210 Madison, and I have a question for you."

"Yes?"

"What was your father's name?"

"Gray. Robert Gray. But he went by Frank."

# CHAPTER TWENTY-THREE

210 Madison Avenue looked the same as it did the last time I saw it. Quiet and unoccupied. The red brick burned adobe red beneath the hot sun, and even with the rain, the yard was succumbing to the heat, showing more brown patches. The For Sale sign had a "Sold" placard pasted across it.

I stood across the street, watching the house, waiting for any signs of life, such as realtors or inspectors. No cars were parked in front, but I knew from experience that someone could still be inside. I stared at the notes I held, specifically the ones with Cal's research about the house. The last owner was R. F. Gray, Edna Mills' father, who was also, apparently, known as Frank Gray. Who was Henri's client.

Before coming over, I had researched R. F. Gray on the Internet. I wanted to know more about this collector that Henri knew. Gray was a well-known name in the Hollywood memorabilia community because of his extensive collection of pre-World War II items. Known to have lived modestly, Gray spent most of his resources on his family and his collection. He had amassed numerous rare posters and props from the movies, and had hundreds of signed pieces – pictures, stills, letters, postcards, and other things. After the death of his wife in 1994, Gray quit purchasing any more collectibles, and a year later sold off what he had.

His collected works garnered millions at a New York auction. He died peacefully in his sleep, right here in Denver.

"What're you doing there?"

I whirled around to see the old, gardening neighbor shamble around from the side of his house. He wheeled a cart piled with tools, peat moss, and a case of flowers in front of him.

"I'm interested in that house," I said, gesturing at 210 Madison Avenue.

He pushed the cart up to a beautiful rose bush and unloaded the bag of dirt as if it were feathers, showing strength that seemed impossible for a man of his fragile appearance. His face was wrinkled with a texture like old parchment. I would've sworn he was born at the beginning of the century – the last century.

"It's sold," he said, matter-of-factly, tipping a tattered straw hat at me.

"I know, but I like it." I shaded my eyes against the glare of the sun.

"Huh," he said, his lips protruding out. His faded denim overalls were at least three sizes too big, and his scrawny arms protruded from a threadbare cotton shirt he wore with the sleeves rolled up to the elbows. "It's just a house."

"Did you know the owner?"

"Frank?" The gums worked, moving his jaws forward and back. "Sure. What a character he was. We used to go fishing together, back in the day. Never did cotton to the movies like he did. Waste of time, if you ask me. I don't even have a television."

"Did you ever see Frank's memorabilia collection?"

"Had the stuff all over the house. But he sold it all."

"I see," I said.

The old man picked up a hand shovel, knelt down, and dug into the peat moss, throwing some of it around the base of the rose bush.

"Thanks for your time," I said, starting back to my car parked around the corner.

"That place is haunted," he said, catching me by surprise. It came out "hanted", like he was from the South. I hadn't detected an accent before, but the longer he talked, the more I distinguished one.

"You don't say," I murmured back at him.

"Ay." He dropped the shovel down and grabbed a pair of pruning shears, and set to work on the bushes. After a moment, when he was sure he had an audience, he scrutinized me with beady eyes. "Yep. Been all kinds of noises there." I took a couple of steps down the front walk. "Mostly at night," he continued with a knowing nod of his head.

"What ghost ever traipsed around in the daytime?" I thought, but only smiled at him.

"And lights," he said. "Lights going on and off."

Great, now we were heading into the UFO arena.

"You best watch for the screams, son."

Now that stopped me. Don't get me wrong, I like a good scary movie, but this was going a little far.

"Screams?"

"One night, I heard 'em." The wrinkles on his face moved as he spoke. "I let Penelope out to do her business." I hoped Penelope was a four-legged critter. "I waited for her on the porch, watching the stars while she ran about the yard. And I heard it." It came out as "heared".

"A scream?"

He nodded.

"Just one?"

"No, wasn't just one. More like two or three. Last one sounded funny. Like the person started to scream, but then it seemed like it got cut in half."

Now he was really giving me the creeps.

"This happened just once?"

"Screaming only happened once." He stopped pruning, set the sheers down, and pulled a blue handkerchief from his pocket, wiping the sweat off his face as he talked. "The lights I've seen a lot."

I pondered what he was telling me. "You wouldn't happen to remember when this was?"

"Why dontcha just ask me, son? 'Course I remember. Been happening for a month now. Couple of times a week."

He bobbed his head up and down thoughtfully.

"Couple of times a week," I repeated, nodding in the same slow manner as the old man. He was rubbing off on me.

"Ay. You best think twice about buying that house."

"It's sold," I said.

"That it is," he mused. "That it is."

>> >> >> >> >>

The moon hung behind clouds and any illumination from streetlights was too far away to make a dent in the dark alley behind Frank Gray's former residence. The closed garages, trash cans, dumpsters, trees and bushes melded into the framework of the darkness, and the alley seemed alive with spooks.

"Why exactly do you need me?" Cal asked as we got out of Cal's car.

"I can't do it myself."

"I could've shown you."

"What else do you have to do on a Friday night?"

Cal rolled his eyes at me.

"Come on." I eased down the alley, with Cal right behind me, so close his black boots nearly clipped my heels with every footfall.

"Are you going to complain all night?" I retorted in a whisper.

"Maybe."

We walked in silence for a few moments. Our shoes made a crunching noise on the rocky pavement. A car drove by one block over, but since it was almost midnight, we heard little else but the sound of our breathing and our clothes rustling like leaves in a breeze.

"This is crazy," Cal whispered.

"Maybe," I murmured over my shoulder.

"I'm hotter than hell."

He wore black jeans, a long sleeve black T-shirt, and a dark wool hat, what he called the "Navy Seal" look, inspired by an outfit I'd worn on a previous case.

"Why'd you dress for winter?" I had on black khaki pants and a black short sleeve shirt. Much more comfortable. I was sweating, but I doubt as much as Cal.

"I wanted to blend in."

That would make a good excuse for the Neighborhood Watch committee. *But really, I always wear wool in July.*

We passed a high wooden fence.

"ARF. ARF. ARF." The deep, heavy barking of a big dog split the stillness, accompanied by snarls, low and menacing.

Cal and I emitted curses at the same time. All thoughts of stealth left us, and simultaneously, our legs propelled us quickly down the alley until we halted directly behind 210 Madison Avenue. I peeked through the slits in the wooden fence to make sure I'd found the right house.

"Oh, I'm going to die," Cal wheezed, holding a hand over his heart. "Please God, just take me now."

"Shut up," I gasped, crouching down. "It was just a dog."

"Man, the police are going to come for sure. What will I tell my mother?"

I reached out and grabbed Cal's sleeve and yanked for all I was worth. He stumbled and fell to his knees half on top of me.

"Will you be quiet?" I hissed into his ear. "We haven't broken any laws, you idiot."

With a querulous jerk of his arm, Cal extracted himself from me, and sat back on his haunches. But he was mute.

Down the alley, the dog continued to bark.

I eased partway to my feet and peered in the direction we'd come. I couldn't see anything in the gloom.

After five minutes of waiting and watching, the dog finally stopped his barking. I peered into the darkness. The only thing I could see, other than shadows, was Cal frowning at me.

"Are you all right?" I asked in a low voice.

"Do I *look* all right?"

He crossed his arms over his chest, giving me his best "I'm disgusted" glare.

"You look okay. Like a dog just scared the crap out of you, but okay."

The line of his lips quivered, and then Cal broke into a smile.

"Why do I let you talk me into this stuff?" he asked softly.

"Admit it, you love it."

I glanced up and down the alley once more before grabbing the handle on the gate. I pulled it back and the gate swung open with a low creak of the hinges. I darted into the backyard with Cal so close I could smell the pepperoni pizza he'd had for dinner.

We waited a second, and didn't hear anything.

"Let's go."

We made a mad dash through the grass to the back porch of the house. Once there, we checked for signs of life, but the yard and surrounding houses were as still as tombstones.

"You're on," I said, holding the back screen door open.

Cal stepped around me and stooped down to examine the lock on the back door.

"This doesn't look hard."

He pulled a tiny set of tools from the pocket of his jeans, extracted a couple of thin pieces of metal, and inserted them into the lock mechanism.

"One of these days I need to teach you how to do this," Cal muttered.

"Fine, but not tonight."

"I must be crazy to be doing this."

Cal fiddled with the tools for less than thirty seconds. I kept my eyes peeled on the backyard, but nothing moved.

"There," he grunted. The back door opened. I braced myself for the screeching of an alarm, but nothing happened.

We both stood in the doorway, unsure of our next move.

"Okay, Sherlock," Cal finally whispered. "Lead the way."

# CHAPTER TWENTY-FOUR

Cal stepped aside. I flipped on a tiny flashlight and tiptoed into the small kitchen. Cal followed, pulling the door shut behind him.

"Lock it," I said, speaking in a low voice. "No use having someone surprise us."

"Good idea." Cal turned the lock on the knob.

"Now." He mimicked my hushed tone. "What exactly are we looking for?"

I flashed the light around the kitchen. The room was large, with a long laminate counter against the back wall and a shallow stainless steel sink. Over the sink a small window overlooked the backyard. The cupboards were the flat, pine style of the late '50's, with brass handles, and the wallpaper reminded me of something out of the '70's. The beam of light picked up faded spots on the walls where pictures once hung.

"We're looking for any signs of Frank Gray's memorabilia collection."

I hurried to the window and lowered a set of blinds so no one could see in. There was nothing in the house to absorb the sound, so our voices echoed off the walls as we talked.

"But the collection was sold."

"True, but I think there may be more hidden here," I said.

"Why?" Cal started opening the cupboards.

"I doubt anyone would've missed anything so obvious," I said as I watched him check the empty cabinets.

"I'm thirsty," Cal retorted. "I'm looking for a glass." He pawed inside a cabinet.

"Okay, Einstein, and if you find a glass, what are you going to drink?"

Cal eyed me as if I were stupid. "Water," he said, pointing at the sink.

"The house has been empty for a long time. I doubt the water's even on."

"Oh."

"Come on."

I smothered a laugh and walked into the living room. Nothing but bare white walls and well-worn tan carpet. A cursory examination of the rest of the main floor proved the same. Cal followed me around like a puppy, nervously biting his lip as he watched me.

"There has to be more memorabilia here," I said, strolling down a narrow hall from the bedrooms.

"If you aren't going to find stuff in the kitchen cabinets, what makes you think you'll find it in the bedrooms?" Cal asked sarcastically.

"I'm looking for a place to hide it, like behind a false door or something," I said.

"Why would it be in the house at all?"

"Ned Healy's notes about the Oscars matched with Henri's notes."

"What?"

"When I was at Ned's house, I found a notepad in his office that had some random Oscar information scribbled on it," I said as I opened the closet door in a small bedroom. "You know, just trivia things about the statuette, how much it weighs and stuff like that. I didn't think too much about it at the time, but later I found the same Oscar description on some notes I saw at Henri's shop."

"But what does that prove, other than that both men had researched how the Academy Award was made?"

"Their descriptions both included the same errors!" I stopped and turned the light on him. "I didn't even notice at first, but then I compared their descriptions to the official design of the Oscar. Ned and Henri's descriptions of the Oscar design aren't correct."

"Maybe they both checked the same website for the information." Cal held a hand up to block the light shining in his face.

"I could see Ned doing that, but not Henri. This is his business, remember? Henri would know exactly how an Oscar statuette is designed."

Cal shrugged.

"Don't you see?" I couldn't contain my excitement. "Henri said the fake Oscar that Frank Gray owned, the replica created to look like Barry Fitzgerald's headless Oscar, had *one small thing* wrong with it. How could it be that both Ned and Henri had notes about an Oscar statuette with one item wrong in the design, and both of their notes describe the exact same anomaly? Because they were both looking at the same statue," I said with emphasis. "And how did Ned even get his hands on it? Because he got it from Frank Gray's collection."

"How?"

"Everything points to this house. It's too coincidental that Ned Healy, who seemingly had no interest in the movies and no money to buy expensive memorabilia, had what I think is an original *Maltese*

*Falcon* poster, had notes about a fake Oscar in his office, and was also the real estate agent with a contract on a house that just happened to be owned by one of the premier collectors of Hollywood memorabilia."

For the first time I detected a knowing look on Cal's face. What I'd been saying was finally making sense.

I continued. "More stuff has to be here someplace, and I think that's why Ned was killed. He found part of the collection in the house, and told someone else about it – someone who didn't want to share the wealth with Ned."

"But why didn't the family find the collection when Gray died?"

"I called Edna Mills, Gray's daughter, and she said her dad sold off everything before he died, and she doesn't remember a headless Oscar being sold, or any Humphrey Bogart posters. But she admitted she didn't know what all her dad had. If I'm right, there's got to be more stuff around here somewhere that the family didn't find when they cleared out the house."

"And you think the headless replica given to Gray is the same statue with the anomaly that Ned and Henri described?"

"Uh-huh."

"But if Ned had the Oscar, how did Henri know about it?"

"I don't know. Maybe Ned showed it to Henri and then brought it back here. Maybe he didn't take it from the house, but someone else did. Maybe he told Samantha about the stuff and *she* stole items from the collection. But I'll never know if I'm right unless I can find out if there's more of the collection here."

Cal stared at me for the longest time, then said, "You're crazy."

"Uh-huh."

I stalked into the hallway and aimed the flashlight at the ceiling.

"There's an attic. Help me get up there."

Cal stooped down and locked his fingers together, forming a loop. I stepped into his cupped hands and he boosted me up with a grunt.

"Hurry up," he said through gritted teeth.

"I am."

I used one arm and balanced against the wall, and with the other popped the attic cover back. I clenched the light between my teeth and grabbed the framework with both hands. I hoisted myself up and Cal seized my legs, pushing me further up. Once my head and shoulders cleared the opening, I shined the light into the attic. I didn't see anything but insulation and cobwebs.

"Nothing," I said, again holding onto the framework. Cal let go of my legs and I dropped to the floor.

"Why not ask Edna to let you in?"

I brushed dirt off my hands. "I tried that. I finally 'fessed up to who I was, but she didn't believe me."

"The ace detective is foiled again," Cal said. "Tune in next week for the exciting conclusion."

I glared at him. "She believed me when I said I was a detective. She just didn't believe that there was more to her dad's collection, and she wouldn't agree to let me in the house."

"So you decided to throw caution out the door, ignore the law, and break into the house yourself."

"If Jack Healy could see me now," I said.

"Why?"

"I told him I wasn't too hip on bending the law."

"No, but you're okay with breaking it," Cal chuckled. "But what if you don't find anything?"

"I don't know." A sinking feeling hit me in the gut. What if I was wrong? I dismissed the thought. "Let's take a look downstairs."

I'd seen a door off the kitchen when we came in, so we traipsed back through the house and took the creaky wooden steps down to the basement. My pencil-thin flashlight created a tunnel of illumination in front of us, but outside its range was total blackness.

"This place gives me the creeps," Cal said.

The longer we were in the house, the more I had to agree. The silence was overpowering.

At the bottom of the stairs, I turned left into a large family room. A built-in bookcase lined one wall, empty and coated with a layer of dust. As I panned the light around the room, I saw indentations in the carpet where a couch and a television stand had been.

"Let's see what else is here." I started for a hallway at the end of the room.

"What was that?" Cal suddenly whispered.

I stopped short. "What?"

"I thought I heard something."

We stood motionless, the flashlight cutting a swatch of light between us. I could barely make out Cal's face. His eyes were open wide, and his lips were drawn in a tight line.

"The flashlight!" Cal hissed.

I switched it off. Darkness enveloped us.

"I don't hear anything," I said after a minute, turning the flashlight back on. "It must've been a car."

Cal shrugged. "Must've been."

I moved down the hall. Cal shuffled along behind me, his breathing ragged.

"Nothing but a laundry room and storage," I said. I searched everywhere, but couldn't find anything that seemed like a hiding place.

A tinny melody suddenly interrupted the silence.

"What the..." I leaped backward, slamming into an old washing machine. It clanked with a loud, hollow sound.

"A phone," Cal said, a second ring coming from inside his pants pocket.

I shined the beam in his face. "Who the hell is calling you at this hour?"

"How do you know it's my cell phone?" he asked, oblivious to the ringing.

"Because my ringer's on mute," I nearly yelled.

"Oh." He used one hand to block the light and checked the phone with the other. "Just a hacker buddy," he said lightly, punching buttons. "I'll shut it off for now."

"Good idea." I glared at him.

"Reed, let's get out of here." Cal edged back into the main room. "We've been here too long."

"Okay, I'm coming." I wasn't ready to give up. "The stuff has to be here someplace."

"Maybe you're wrong."

We stood in the family room, watching as the flashlight illuminated bleak cement walls that had been painted white. In desperation I shined the light on the ceiling.

"You know, there's nothing wrong with the foundation. At least not that I can see," I mused.

"What?"

"Garrett Owens was right. He got talked into making claims for needless repairs." I gestured with the flashlight where the walls met the ceiling. "There aren't any cracks in the foundation, or anywhere else."

Cal was over by the stairs, ready to go up. "Come on."

I moved the light around. "Wait a second."

"Reed."

"Hold on." I approached the bookcases and paced back along the floor to the opposite wall.

"What are you doing?"

I turned around and surveyed the room. "It doesn't add up." Cal came back into the room. "The front of the house goes further than this." I walked the space again. "This room is too narrow."

"A crawl space?" Cal hypothesized.

I stared at him in the gloom. We both turned our attention to the wall with the bookcases.

"It looks solid." I tugged at the shelves.

"Here, do this." Cal began tapping on the wood. "See if it sounds hollow."

I watched him work the length of the wall, knocking every foot or so. Each tap sounded the same to me.

"Well?" I asked when he finished.

"I can't tell," he said sheepishly.

"Keep looking."

We started at one end of the wall and meticulously surveyed every inch of the bookcases, searching for signs of hinges, a door, or a hidden latch, anything that would indicate there was a room on the other side.

"Guess nothing's there," Cal said.

"I must be wrong," I finally admitted defeat. "It's just that everything seemed to make sense."

Cal placed a hand on my shoulder. "Don't give up, buddy. Maybe your theory's right, but the stuff is somewhere else."

"Maybe." I stared down at the floor.

"Let's get out of here."

I turned to follow Cal and tripped on a piece of the carpet that lay unevenly. I landed on my knees and the flashlight went skittering across the floor. "Wow. Someone needs to stretch this better," I grunted. I crawled to where the light lay in the corner. "Garrett Owens should've asked for a carpet allowance."

I picked up the flashlight and noticed that the edge of the carpet, right in the corner, was not tacked down well.

"Wait a second."

I tugged at the carpet, pulling it back. Cal held it and I aimed the beam on the floor. The pool of light exposed a trap door.

# CHAPTER TWENTY-FIVE

"Bingo," I said.

Cal grinned. "Help me with this carpet," he wheezed. "It's getting heavy."

I set the flashlight down and we pulled the carpet away from the trap door.

"It was well hidden," I said, again shining the light on the door. An iron handle shaped like a ring, and large hinges, were both sunk into the wood so no indentation was created in the carpet. Unless you knew what to look for, or tripped on the carpet like I'd just done, you might never find the door.

"Wonder what's in there?" Cal mused. "Maybe a food cellar, with canned peaches and stuff like that. My grandmother had a cellar like that."

I stared at him in disbelief.

"Don't want you to get your hopes up," Cal explained.

"Only one way to find out," I said.

I fiddled with the handle until I could grasp it. I lifted the door, straining under its weight. "The whole thing must be made of iron," I said with a gasp. I finally hoisted the door up. It fell open with a thud. I pointed the light into the opening and saw a wooden ladder. I stuck my head down. A short tunnel led to a dark door.

"Spooky," Cal said, peering over my shoulders. "You go down. I'll stay here."

"Right." I swung a leg around and started gingerly down the ladder. "You wait here in the dark."

Cal's face turned pale. "On second thought, I'll come with you."

"I thought you might," I called up as I reached the bottom. I shined the light up so Cal could see. In less than five seconds, he was beside me.

The tiny passageway, covered in pine planks, was barely wide enough for us to pass through. The temperature had dropped a few degrees, and a slight shift in the air indicated some kind of venting system. A heavy layer of dust covered the floor, but I could easily make out footprints.

"Someone's been in here recently," I said, motioning at the disturbed area.

I crossed to the door and pushed. It swung inward with a sigh, like it hated to be imposed upon.

I stepped into the room and stopped in amazement.

The room was the size of small bedroom, with all four walls and ceiling covered in light wood siding. Metals shelves leaned against two of the walls, and a third wall had a few wooden crates stacked on each other. A framed poster hung on the fourth wall.

"Wow," Cal said as he edged around me and gazed at the poster. Charlie Chaplin stared back at him, from *City Lights*, his feature length movie from 1931. "This is in beautiful shape."

I wasn't looking at the poster. I was gawking at the shelves. Specifically at two gold statues that gleamed in the eerie glow of the flashlight.

I picked one up and studied it.

"Luise Rainer," Cal read over my shoulder. "Best actress in a supporting role, 1937."

He gently lifted the other statue and blew dust off of it. "Man, these are heavy."

"Almost seven pounds," I said. I stared at the Oscar. My mind whirled with all it was seeing.

"Ray Milland. Best Actor in a lead role, 1945," Cal said. He turned the statue around, examining every detail of it. "I can't believe I'm touching an Oscar."

I set down the statue I held, drawn to boxes on the shelves. I popped the lid off one. Inside was a stack of 8x10 publicity stills for a number of actors. Each was in a protective cover, and most were signed. There was Greta Garbo, John Wayne, Grace Kelly, Frank Sinatra. The list went on and on.

I pulled my camera from my pocket and began videoing the room. "No one will believe this."

I opened another box that had smaller lobby cards with everything from Judy Garland's *The Wizard of Oz* to *Public Enemy* with James Cagney. A third box contained tins of movie reels. I read the label. *In The Park*.

"If this is an original copy of the film, it's priceless," I gasped.

"*In The Park*," Cal said. "Never heard of it."

"It's one of Charlie Chaplin's early movies, when he worked at Essaney Studios. It's not like there are tons of copies lying around."

Cal cocked an eyebrow. "I see what you mean about it being priceless."

I lifted the lids off two other boxes. They were empty.

"This is incredible," I said. "There must be hundreds of items here."

Cal nodded.

I filmed items on the other shelves. A number of screenplays sat in binders. I flipped open *It Happened One Night*. "This has notes in the margin. I wonder if it's Clark Gable or Claudette Colbert's handwriting?"

"And they would be?" Cal looked at me to complete the sentence.

'They starred in the movie."

"Oh."

"Wait." I found a piece of paper inside that had a description of the script. "It says the writing is by Frank Capra, that it was his personal script."

"And he would be?"

"The director."

"How do you know all that?" Cal, who knew almost everything about almost everything, didn't know much about the movies.

"Remember who you're talking to," I said.

"Oh yeah. The movie buff. How has this stuff stayed in such good shape?" Cal asked. He stood back while I continued to flip through binders.

"I don't know. There must be some way that Gray kept this room temperature-controlled, although that film should be protected better than this. Who knows how long Frank had this stuff stashed away." Some sort of environmental control would explain why the room didn't have a dank, musty smell I would've expected from a sub-basement.

"I'll bet you're right," Cal said. "Ned found this little treasure trove and saw a way out of his financial troubles. But who else knew about it?"

"I don't know. Samantha, another friend, a realtor associate? Someone who got Ned out of the way, and has been coming in here and taking the stuff, then getting Henri to appraise and sell it." I couldn't believe the number of screenplays that were sitting on the shelves, many of them with scrawled notes by an actor or director. Frank Gray must've collected them for years, because I found scripts for movies from the '30's through the '80's.

"Uh Reed..." Cal's voice had a quiver in it.

"No wait, I'm on a roll here." I rummaged through more stuff. "So the guy, or woman, whoever, comes in here at odd times, that's why the neighbor saw lights and heard noises. Whoever knew about this had to get things cleared out in a hurry because the house is on the market to sell. Once the new owners move in, there's no chance of getting to the stuff. Not without a lot more hassle."

"Reed."

"I've got more work to do, though. I have to find out who Ned told about the collection..." I turned around and froze.

Cal was standing with his arms over his head, the classical "I'm being held up" stance. Even in the muted light I could see the fear etched on his face. Behind him was the house inspector that I'd seen leaving by the back door a few days earlier. I couldn't see a gun, but I knew he had one rammed into Cal's back.

"Well, well, well." The inspector pushed Cal toward me. "Looks like the cat is out of the bag."

Cal stumbled into me. As I caught him, I set the camera onto a shelf. Cal shook uncontrollably.

"Give me the flashlight." The inspector held out his hand. "Slowly.

You don't want to make me nervous."

I carefully gave it to him. I waited for him to ask about the camera, but he didn't. In the dimness, he must not have seen me holding it. I hoped it was still recording, but I didn't want to glance at it to find out.

"I told you we should've left," Cal whispered.

"You think you're pretty smart, figuring this all out," the guy sneered, shining the light in our faces. He had done something to his hair. It was darker. I squinted against the glare, aware of his cold brown eyes.

"A little late to be doing inspections, don't you think?" I asked in an even tone.

"Inspections?" A puzzled expression formed on his hard features. "Oh yeah, the other day." He shrugged. "You assumed I was an inspector when I left the house, so I went along with it. You know, if you act like you belong, no one will question you."

I'd aspired to that philosophy many a time myself, but it had never bit me in the butt like it was now – my ass seems to get a lot of the brunt of my detective work.

"Okay, you're not an inspector. Then who are you?" He swung the gun toward me. I swallowed what felt like a sock in my throat.

"You don't have this all figured out? You were on a roll there, explaining everything to your pal, I might as well let you finish the story. I'll just wait for the ending. Your ending."

Cal shuddered. "Where's *your* gun?" he hissed to me.

The man tensed.

"At the office, locked in the closet," I whispered back.

The guy relaxed and a smile crept across his face. He snickered.

"Good place for it," Cal said, still talking in an undertone.

"Well," I shrugged. Now was not the time to get into my lack of gun prowess.

"I should never have let you talk me into this," Cal muttered. "I like staying in my house. I don't need to go anywhere. I'm not like you. I don't need adventure in my life."

"Shut up," the fake inspector said, raising the gun higher. Still pointed at me.

"I can work, do everything in the safety of my own home," Cal continued, oblivious to the warning. His voice rose. "But no-o-o-o-! You had to have help, had to have me come down here. Now look at us."

"Shut up!" the inspector and I yelled at the same time.

Cal blanched, then opened his mouth. Nothing came out, so he clamped his jaw shut, crossed his arms, and alternated between glaring at me and our captor.

"Let me handle this," I said out of the corner of my mouth. I silently cursed the fact that we'd broken into the house. If the police came – and how would they since neither Cal nor I were in a position to call them – how would we explain being down here in the first place?

"Uh- huh," Cal murmured back. "You're handling it really well."

Little veins were popping out of our captor's forehead, and he barely controlled his rage. "I told you to be quiet." He spoke each word carefully, taking a step forward and waving the gun at Cal, who began sweating profusely.

"You're a friend of Ned's, right?" I asked, trying to diffuse some of the guy's anger.

He stared at Cal, daring a confrontation, but Cal was too smart, or scared, to move.

"Finishing the story?" he finally said to me. The gun dropped a little, still menacingly aimed at us, but not as aggressively. He took a deep breath and let it out slowly. "Okay, I'll play along. I knew Ned."

"You're..." I said, scrambling to find the name, "Dominic Saunders. The second buyer for this house."

The surprised look told me I was right.

"It's Dom," he said. "How'd you figure that out?"

"It's the only thing that makes sense," I said. "You're the only one, other than Ned, who stands to benefit from Garrett Owens losing the contract on this house."

"Who?" He genuinely appeared to not to know the name.

"Garrett Owens," I said. "He lives in the same apartment complex that you did, Mountain View Apartments, and he was the first buyer for this house."

"Never heard of him," Dom said.

"It was just coincidence that two buyers for the same house lived in the same apartment complex?"

Dom shrugged. "Guess so." But we both knew he was lying. He locked eyes with me. "You know, you're smarter than you look."

Cal made a sound between a cough and a laugh.

"Thanks," I said automatically, not sure if Dom meant to compliment or insult me.

"I should've finished you off when I had the chance."

I didn't like the edge in his voice. My hands grew damp with sweat. "At the office," I said, realization dawning on me. "You're the one who attacked me."

"You were getting too close. I couldn't have you screwing things up." He paused. "Like you are."

"How did you know who I was, or where to find me?"

"Do you remember when you were at that movie shop the other day? I saw you in the back."

It had only been a little over a week ago, but it seemed like forever.

"I came in with some stuff I took from here, and I went to the old man to appraise it. While we were talking, I saw the poster you were looking at. *The Maltese Falcon*. Hell, I didn't even know about the movie before I saw this stuff, but Ned researched all that crap. And I could tell by the old wooden frame that Ned had stolen it from here, because it's like all the others from the collection. I'd told Ned to leave everything here until we got ready to sell it, but he wouldn't listen. And then here's this guy," he gestured with the gun at me, "you – the same guy I'd caught snooping around this house, with Ned's poster at that shop. I had to know how you got your hands on the thing. At first I told myself you might be someone who knew about Frank Gray. No big deal. But that didn't explain how you got the poster. You had to be connected with Ned somehow. So I followed you." He let out a gruff laugh. "Man, was I surprised when I found out you were a detective. Just my luck. I saw Ned's brother with you, so I figured you were looking into Ned's death. Once I saw you around here, I knew I had to get rid of you before you ruined things."

"You attacked Henri," I guessed again.

"The old French guy? He called me and accused me of having a stolen Oscar," Dom said, clearly irritated. "I thought since it was damaged, it would be worthless. How the nutty old guy knew I'd stolen the thing…" his voice trailed off.

"So you tried to get rid of him." I felt fury competing with my fright.

Dom nodded. "He was going to call the police. Too bad. He really knew his stuff."

"And you killed Ned, too." Cal spoke with an anger I hadn't heard before. Fear was doing some strange things to the man.

"Getting rid of Ned was easy," Dom grunted. "He was such a wimp. Whining about how much his life sucked. How he missed that bitch of an ex-wife. Why someone would weep and moan about a selfish little tramp like that?"

"You've known Ned for a long time," I said, trying to piece everything together, at the same time trying to find something in the room that might help us escape.

"A few years. Long enough to know that he was better off without Samantha." Dom smirked. "C'mon, if she would sleep with me while she was married to him, what kind of a wife was she?"

"What kind of a friend were you?" Cal spat out.

"I never said I was Ned's friend," Dom said, eerily calm. "I said I knew him. I knew Samantha better." He leered at some passionate memory of Samantha. "Man, she was easy. Problem was, she thought she'd fallen in love with me. Yeah, right. Way too high maintenance for me, always going on about how Ned screwed her over, how he still had stuff of hers, stuff that meant something. Man, I got tired of that."

"How did you meet Ned?" I asked.

"He'd called me for electrical work, originally on his house – that's how I met Samantha – then he referred others to me. Then he had me work at some of the houses he had for sale, like this one. And man, did he brag about this place. He couldn't keep his mouth shut about all this memorabilia." Dom chewed on his lip thoughtfully. "You know, I wondered why he would tell me about this. I think he knew about

Samantha and me, because he kept saying that she'd soon see things differently, that he had a way to make some big bucks. I kept asking Ned what he'd found, and he finally showed me this room. Said he discovered it, but not until after he had a buyer for the home. He needed to get the buyer out of the way, and he offered to share the memorabilia with me if I'd help him."

"Why not steal the stuff yourself? Why bother working with Ned?" I asked. Keep him talking.

"Ned steal? You're joking." A crooked smile spread across Dom's face. "Ned wasn't about to go that far. No, he figured he could fudge things and get the buyer to lose the contract, and then I could buy the place. Once I owned it, we could clear out this room, and then put the house back on the market. He said he would've bought it himself, but he didn't have the money, and it would look suspicious."

"That's a lot of work."

The smile widened. He waved his arm in an arc. "This is a lot of stuff. And worth a lot of money."

"But you didn't plan on *your* contract falling through," I said.

His brown eyes narrowed. "No, I didn't. Neither did Ned. We talked about what to do, and I said I was going to steal the stuff out of the house, the hell with his plan. I had the combination to the lock box, so I let myself in. But he came by and found me here. We fought." Dom shook his head in disgust. "Ned yelled and hollered at me." I thought about the old man across the street hearing the screams. "I backed off and let him think he'd won. The idiot wanted to try and find another buyer who would go along. Like we could chance that. Besides, then we'd have to split things three ways."

"And since you weren't really Ned's friend, he was expendable," I continued to prod him, buying time until I could formulate a plan of escape. Given our circumstances, I was going to need a lot of time.

"You think I'm so stupid I would let him get more people involved? Ned was a fool for telling me about all this."

"How'd you do it?" I asked. I was fighting a feeling of despair because I didn't see any way out. Dom blocked the doorway, and there was no other exit. Our goose was cooked.

"He came over to discuss yet another plan to steal this stuff and I got him drunk. Spiked a few drinks with some Seconal. I used his car and drove us up into the mountains. He slept the whole way up to the trail head. I talked him into the ride, but he was so wasted I don't think he really knew where he was." Dom stopped as if remembering. "The hardest part was helping him keep his balance. He must've fallen a dozen times. But I got him to that side trail and pushed him, right over the edge."

It was not a pretty thought. Cal shuddered. I winced.

"I rode on back to the city. Took a while, but I like to ride."

"And it cleared the way for you to steal all this memorabilia," I said.

Dominic beamed at his resourcefulness. "Well, enough story time," he said, now all business. "It's time to take care of you two, and get the rest of this stuff out of here."

"What are you going to do to us?"

"An accident." Dom thought about this. "Two guys find this great hiding place, but get trapped down here. Buried alive."

I heard Cal swallow. Or maybe I heard myself.

Dom yanked some rope from his back pocket. "What I want to know is how you figured it out," he said to me.

"The Oscar," I said. "Let me show you what I mean." I carefully moved to the shelf where the two treasured statuettes sat, waiting for the sound of Dom's gun to explode with each step I took. "Right here," I said, picking up the Best Supporting Oscar. "You see that?" I held the Oscar up, taking a few steps toward Dom. He moved over and peered down where my finger was resting on the base of the statue.

"What?"

"This."

I held it up to show Dom something, but instead swung the little gold man squarely at his face. It happened so fast, and unexpectedly, that Dom didn't have time to move. The marble base caught him right on the bridge of his nose.

His eyes widened in surprise and pain. The gun exploded, and the room filled with the echo of the blast. At the same time I heard a scream that I wasn't sure came from Dom, Cal, or me. It might have been all of us.

The room reeled in eerie shadows as the flashlight hit the floor with a metallic clunk. The room went completely dark.

"Reed!" Cal shouted from my left.

Close to my feet I heard moaning and cursing. "You broke my nose," Dom groaned nearby.

I fell to my knees, pawing around on the floor, searching for the flashlight and the gun. At the same time I was aware of my sore ribs screaming at me.

A cool piece of metal suddenly connected with my cheek. I heard a click.

"Move and I'll kill you," Dom hissed at me.

I froze, knowing that his anger and pain mixed into a dangerous cocktail.

"Tell your friend to find the flashlight, and if he does anything crazy, you get a bullet right in the face."

I had an absurdly comical urge to ask why I should tell Cal something that he had just heard Dom say, but resisted. Fear was doing funny things to me.

Something like the sound of a whip disturbed the air.

Thunk!

In a split instance, I realized a number of things. The cool touch of the metal left my face. At the same time, a thump broke the quiet, and I presumed that Dom had fallen to the floor. Then I comprehended that one side of *my* face, not Dom's, was on the floor, and that the left side of my head felt like a hammer had pounded on it.

I heard the same funny whistling noise in the air and another thump.

"Ugh," Dom moaned. Another thump.

Then silence.

"Reed?" Cal whispered.

"Where are you?" I was still immobile.

"Hold on."

Cal scooted around, making shuffling noises as he scoured his hands across the floor.

"Here we go," he said.

A burst of light sprang out of the darkness, wobbling crazily. I let my eyes adjust.

Cal was on his knees by the door, the flashlight in one shaky hand, and a broken gold statue in the other. Dom was lying on the floor between us, face down, a tiny rivulet of blood running down his right temple.

"Is he dead?" Cal murmured.

"I don't know." I pulled myself up and frantically scanned the room. The gun was half-under one of the metal shelves. I snatched it up and aimed it at Dom's inert body.

"Check him," I said.

"You check him," Cal retorted.

"I've got to keep him covered. Unless you want the gun." I touched my head while we talked. A large lump had formed above my ear. Beaned on the head twice in one case.

Cal muttered threats at me under his breath, but eased forward and touched a finger to Dom's neck. "There's a pulse." He sat back and sighed. "Guess I knocked him out cold."

"Take that rope and tie him up," I ordered.

This time Cal worked feverishly. He tossed me the flashlight and set to work with Dom's own rope, trussing him up before he regained consciousness.

"That was a good shot," I said after Cal finished. I picked up the damaged Oscar. "Let me ask you, how did you know who you were hitting? I mean, since you couldn't see anything."

"It was dark," Cal said slowly.

"Uh-huh," I prompted him to continue.

"I heard his voice."

"Yes?"

"And I swung at it."

"And hit me."

"I swung again and hit him."

"I see," I said. "But how did you know that, even if you did hit him first, that his finger wouldn't accidentally pull the trigger?"

Cal shrugged. "I, uh…"

"I could've been killed!"

"I thought you were him."

"Do I sound like him?"

Cal stared at me. "If I didn't do it, we probably both would've been killed."

I burst into laughter, feeling the adrenaline waste out of my body. "Touché. A headache is worth it."

"We'd better call the police." Cal grabbed his cell phone.

"Uh," I hesitated. "First, how are you going to get a signal down here? Second, if you call the police, Watson, how are you going to explain why we're here?"

Cal groaned. "So what do we do?"

I contemplated the still form at our feet. "Let's get out of here, and we'll call the police later and tell them about Dom."

"An anonymous phone call."

I nodded. "Not that creative, but it'll do."

"But then no one knows that he killed Ned Healy."

I pointed at the camera. "It's been recording the whole time. At least I think it has." I grabbed it off the shelf and pushed a button. "It never shut off." I breathed a relieved sigh as I hit a couple more buttons. Cal and I then watched as the video showed Dom standing in the dim room pointing a gun. Sometimes he moved out of the camera's eye, but it didn't matter. The audio was perfect, capturing his confession for all to hear. "It's all recorded. Jack can take that to the police."

"Will that work?"

"It's the best we can do, given the circumstances." I pursed my lips. "Unless we want to explain being here."

Cal shook his head vigorously. "Oh no. And don't use 'we' like that. This was your idea."

"Okay, okay." I held up a hand. "C'mon, we'd better get out of here."

"It really is a shame," Cal said sadly.

"What?"

"The Oscar." Cal picked up the little gold statue from the floor. It was the one he'd used to hit Dom and me. It was missing its head and upper body, the edges of the remains jagged as broken glass. "I ruined a valuable piece of Hollywood memorabilia."

"No you didn't."

"Huh?"

I took the damaged Oscar and turned it on its side. "This one is fake, just like the Barry Fitzgerald replica." I pointed to the base of the statue. "Remember the description in the notes? How the base is made of marble, and looks like a reel of film? After 1928, the reel had five slots, for the five original branches of the Academy. It remained the same until the '40's when they added more slots to the reel. See this Oscar? It's supposedly from 1936, so the base should have only five slots, but it has more slots than that. It's a fake."

"So that's what you meant."

I smiled. "There's actually one more thing that tells me this Oscar is a fake."

"And that would be?"

"Look at the inscription."

"Luise Rainer. Best Supporting Actress, 1937," Cal read. He looked up at me. "So?"

"Up until 1943, they gave supporting actors a plaque, not a statuette."

"I didn't know that."

"Can I mark that down?" I grinned. "Something Cal didn't know."

"Ha, ha. But why would Frank Gray have fake Oscars in his collection? Why not go after real ones?"

"Maybe it was another joke by his wife," I said, and reminded Cal about the joke Gray's wife had pulled on him. I made a mental note to ask Henri if he knew about a second fake Oscar. "And unless I miss the mark, that other Oscar on the shelf is real."

Cal let out a whistle. "Wow. This guy had a truly amazing collection."

"Think of all the stuff he already sold."

"Who would've thought."

# CHAPTER TWENTY-SIX

Once Cal and I let ourselves out of 210 Madison Avenue, we snuck back to the 4-Runner and called the police from a pay phone at a nearby gas station. Again, not very creative, but it did the trick. We waited a block down from the house until we saw a police cruiser stop and park out front. Cal, who made the call, had thoughtfully told the 911 operator that the back door of the house was unlocked, and when the officers made their way around to the back yard, we drove back to my place. I dropped Cal off at his car and parked the 4-Runner in the garage. I slowly made my way upstairs to my condo, popped a couple of aspirin to ward off the headache I had, and got ready for bed. The alarm clock read 3:10 when I finally slipped under the covers.

» » » » »

The alarm on the nightstand in my bedroom buzzed at ten, but it seemed like my head had just hit the pillow. I didn't even think I'd had time to make a dent in it.

I shut the alarm off, dragged myself into the bathroom and took a long cool shower. I gingerly washed my hair, the bump that Cal had given me throbbing like it had a heartbeat of its own. Once I'd dressed, I plodded into the kitchen and took a couple more aspirin, then prepared a strong batch of coffee.

While I waited for the java to brew I called Jack and asked him to meet me at my office at 12:30, which would give me just enough time to wake up. From the tone in his voice, I could tell Jack was puzzled that I wanted to meet on a Saturday, but he was agreeable.

Two cups of coffee, and then I donned sunglasses and headed outside. A dry heat indicated that the mercury was already high and climbing higher.

On the way to the office, I stopped for a bagel and munched on it as I downloaded the video I'd recorded in the sub-basement.

"...that you did, Mountain View Apartments, and he was the first buyer for this house," I heard myself say. The quality of the recording was decent.

"Never heard of him. You know, you're smarter than you look." Dom said next. Then I heard Cal snorting at the comment. I remembered this part of the conversation – I had just asked Dom if he knew Garrett Owens.

I listened to the entire conversation, right up until Cal and I argued about whom he'd attempted to bean with the Oscar. The camera had shut off when I dropped to the floor after Cal hit me. I breathed a sigh of relief, glad the recording hadn't stopped earlier. Dom's confession sounded crystal clear.

Just at noon, Jack poked his head through the doorway.

"Right on time. Have a seat," I waved him over. I finished typing an email and sent it before turning to Jack. "I'm just taking care of a few things here."

"I hope this meeting means you have some news," Jack said, settling into a seat across from my desk. He crossed one leg over the other, then ran a hand through his hair. His stark white shirt had circles of sweat under the armpits, but otherwise he looked crisp and clean.

I turned the computer monitor around so he could see it. "Listen to this." I clicked on the video and pressed play. Hissing blared out of the speakers, then my voice.

"What's this?" Jack said, staring at me.

"Hold on," I shushed him.

Jack folded his arms and listened. At first he seemed irritated, but as the recording progressed, anger turned to disbelief. When Dom got around to how he had killed Ned, Jack bolted upright in the chair.

"The man talking to us is Dominic Saunders," I said after the video finished. "This happened last night – well, this morning, early."

"How did you get that?" Jack sputtered.

I explained the events of the last evening, concluding with how Cal and I didn't want to face charges ourselves, so we'd left Dom in the basement and called the police anonymously.

"Incredible," Jack said, shaking his head. "But you were the guy who didn't want to break the law."

I felt my cheeks getting hot. "And see what happened when I did. I boxed myself into a corner. I'll send you the video."

"What do I do with this?"

"Show it to the police. It may not be sexy, but it'll get the ball rolling."

"And when they ask about the others on the tape? The voices with Dominic?"

I smiled. "You can tell them you don't know."

"Bend the law." He raised his eyebrows. I fought off a bigger smile.

Jack smiled back, then his face clouded over. "What about the memorabilia?"

I shrugged. "Once the police get involved, I'm sure they'll work with Gray's daughter, Edna, and maybe an insurance company, to catalogue the collection. They'll have to talk to Henri about what he sold, to see if they can recover any of it." I pursed my lips. "Since the house was sold, there might be a fight between Edna and the new owners as to who owns the collection."

"That could get interesting," Jack said.

I glanced at the wall. "I may have to give *The Maltese Falcon* poster back."

"That *would* be too bad," Jack smiled ruefully. "I think you earned it.

"Thanks," I said.

"The thanks goes to you. You found out the truth about Ned's death." A weary sadness settled across Jack's face. He again was the spitting image of Burt Lancaster in *The Killers*. "I knew I was right about Ned. I just wish it made me feel better."

"I know," I said.

He stood up and thanked me. We shook hands. Jack stared at the computer monitor, with Dom frozen on the screen. It was all the validation he needed, with none of the peace he wanted. He shrugged his shoulders, then left.

» » » » »

Soon afterward, I headed to the hospital. Henri's room was quiet, with only the sounds of voices speaking in French breaking through the other noises in a busy building. The good news was that Henri was awake.

"Oh, Reed," Evaline beamed at me as I scooted up a chair and sat down next to her. Henri was propped up in bed, a stack of pillows behind his back.

"You look tired, eh?" Henri said.

"I didn't get much sleep last night," I said. The three of us chatted for a few minutes about Henri's health – improving dramatically, a few problems with his vision, but they expected to send him home soon; the weather – too hot for Evaline, but she would survive; and how much we all hated hospital food – especially the green Jell-O.

"Do you remember what happened? Who attacked you?" I asked the questions as soon as I could politely fit them in.

"I don't remember," Henri said, while Evaline shook her head dejectedly. "I was in the back office, working. Then I wake up here." He seemed disappointed with himself.

"The doctors say a head injury can cause him not to remember," Evaline explained.

"It's okay," I said. "I'm sure the police will find who did this to you." I thought about the taped confession. I had no doubt they would learn the truth.

Evaline excused herself, ostensibly to use the restroom, but I think she knew I wanted to discuss business with Henri. "Henri," I asked, "Do you remember why you called me the other day? When my cell phone wasn't working."

"Ah, yes. I wanted to tell you about the Oscar that man brought into the store. It was the fake one, just like Frank Gray's wife gave him. I called that man about it. I wanted to know how he got it." His face clouded. "Evaline tells me the Oscar was stolen from the shop."

"I'm sure it'll turn up." I paused. "Was that fake Oscar the only one created? Couldn't there be more of them?"

Henri smiled slyly. "Not like those."

"Those?" I cocked an eyebrow at him.

"Ah. I told you Gray had one fake Oscar, yes?" He leaned toward me conspiratorially. "He had two. His wife asked my help in making another. She wanted to know which actor it should be for." His eyes sparkled with mischief. "I suggested she have one made for Luise Rainer, best supporting actress in 1937."

"Knowing there weren't supporting actor *statuettes* back then."

"I knew I couldn't fool you." Henri clapped his hands in delight. "And it didn't fool Gray either. But he thought it was great fun, eh? Fake Oscars intermingled with his real Oscars. What a collection."

Evaline came back in the room. "What is so funny?" she asked. Henri explained, laughing some more. As the saying goes, it was music to my ears.

After a bit more chatting, I stood up to leave. "Thank you for your help, Reed," Henri said.

"My pleasure."

Evaline looked at me with tears in her eyes. "You're a good boy." She patted my cheek.

"You take care of him," I pretended to scold her.

"You must go, yes?" Henri said.

"I've got some other errands. When you're back at the shop, you let me know, and I'll stop by."

Henri smiled weakly. "That's good. We have a Bogart poster for you."

"I can't wait." I gave Evaline's shoulder a squeeze, shook Henri's scrawny hand, and left.

» » » » »

When I returned home that evening, I made a call to Samantha Healy. She didn't return my call until Monday morning. I arranged to meet her at a Starbucks near her house. I arrived early, ordered a drink, and waited.

Samantha strolled through the door like a queen coming to court. She slid her sunglasses off her face, tossed her hair back seductively, and surveyed the room, well aware of the many eyes that were on her. She looked comfortable in khaki shorts and a denim blouse tied in a knot at her waist, exposing her flat, tanned stomach. She spotted me at a small round table and strolled over.

"What's this all about?" The legs of a chair screeched as she pulled it out and sat down across from me. More eyes turned our way. "Why'd you need to see me?"

"Coffee?" I asked, holding up my mocha.

She shook her head. "I really don't have time for this."

"But you came anyway. Must be my charm."

"You threatened me," she said, leaning her elbows on the table.

I sat back in mock horror. "I merely said I had some information about Dominic Saunders that you might like to know."

At the name Samantha paled. "So you mentioned on the phone." She spoke through a slit in her mouth.

I let a long moment hang between us, building the suspense. "It was you who broke into Ned's house, after he died," I said when the tension was just right.

Samantha's jaw dropped. "What? How did... What are you talking about?" she stammered.

"You're not a good liar."

Her cheeks flushed red. She took a couple of deep breaths. "What makes you think I broke into Ned's house? Why would I want to do that?"

"To get something that belonged to you." I resisted a smile.

"How do you know about that?" A few people turned and looked our way.

"Unless you want your dirty laundry aired in public, I'd suggest you keep your voice down," I said softly.

She scooted her chair closer. "Tell me!" she hissed, elbows planted halfway across the table.

"Remember when I came to the house?" She nodded. "You mentioned that Ned didn't have much of anything in the house, just a stupid poster."

"So?"

"You couldn't have known about the poster unless you'd been in Ned's house recently, because he'd just acquired it. That one statement has been eating at me, and then when Dominic told me about your little affair, it came together."

"I don't know what you're talking about." Now she was really lying badly.

"You know Dominic. The electrical guy that Ned hired. You were all over him, at least that's the way Dominic tells it. And he said that you were angry because Ned still had some things of yours."

"My grandmother's brooch. Ned still had it," she said softly.

"And once he was dead, you could get it without any trouble."

"Yes."

"Did you also call the insurance company?"

Samantha's face twisted into an ugly sort of mask. "You've done your research," she said finally. "So what do you want?"

I sat back. "I only wanted to confirm that I was correct. I don't plan on doing anything with the information, but I thought you might like to know that Dominic killed Ned."

"What?" For the first time Samantha was something other than self-absorbed or angry. "Why?"

"I can't reveal that, but you could call Jack."

Samantha stared at me, saying nothing. Then she slumped back in her chair, deflated. "When we divorced, I couldn't stand Ned," she whispered. "But I never wanted him to die."

I gazed back at her. She seemed like a lost puppy, and I actually came close to feeling sorry for her.

I tossed off the last of my mocha latte and stood up. "I hope you find what you're really looking for," I said and walked away. I could feel her eyes boring into my back as I walked out the door.

» » » » »

She looked so different I hardly recognized her. The spiked hair was gone, as was the black makeup, except for a bit of mascara around the eyes. She wore white shorts, a blue blouse, and sandals. Even her posture seemed more cultured.

Erin Abel strolled to a table in the corner and sat down, her book bag thumping loudly as it hit an empty chair near her. She hadn't noticed me sitting off in a corner, watching her come in.

I stood up and made my way through the maze of tables, stopping in front of her. She had her nose in a book. I cleared my throat and she glanced up.

"Oh, the asshole," she said, her voice flat and unimaginative.

"That's right," I said.

"What do you want?"

"May I sit down?"

Erin narrowed her eyes, staring me down. I held the gaze until she finally used her foot under the table to shove an empty chair backwards. I sat down across from her and folded my hands in front of me.

"I don't have anything to say to you," she spat.

"I owe you an apology," I said.

"Damn straight you do," she threw back at me.

"I shouldn't have lied to you," I continued. "But I'd like to make it up to you."

Erin sat up in her chair, wary. "How?"

I pulled a note from my pocket and set it in front of her. She stared at the paper for a second, then stretched her hand out and took it cautiously, as if it might burn her.

"Who's this?" she asked after reading it.

"He's a producer. Mostly commercials, but he's done a few documentaries. He's a friend of mine. I called him earlier today and asked him if he would have any work for a newcomer."

"He owes you one," Erin said bluntly.

I nodded. "Yeah, but he's a good guy. He said he could use some extra help, behind the cameras to start, but maybe more later. It's worth giving him a call."

Erin gazed at the paper, crinkling the edges with her thumb and forefinger. I was about to get up and leave when she spoke again. "Why are you doing this?"

"I owe *you* one," I said. "I shouldn't have gotten your hopes up the way I did." I pushed my chair back and got up. "I hope you make it big."

For the first time, she smiled, and her face was radiant. Well worth the price of admission. I told her so.

"Thanks," she said, blushing. "And thanks for this," she held up the note.

I smiled back. There were tears in her eyes. Happy tears. It made my Monday.

» » » » »

"Hey Reed, how ya doing?" Deuce said to me when I returned home late that afternoon. He was slouched back in a lounge chair on the porch, a can of Pepsi in his hand. His front door was open and the groovy sounds of reggae wafted out to us. "I'm waiting for Ace to get home. Hot enough for ya?"

"Yep." I sat down on the steps and stretched my legs out.

"You finished work for the day?"

I nodded.

"You want a Pepsi?"

"Sure."

He went inside and returned shortly with a cold soda.

"We're gonna play pool later tonight. You interested?"

"Maybe," I said. "I'm kind of tired."

"You need any more help on the case?"

"No, I wrapped things up today."

A funny look crossed his face, a mix of happiness and disappointment. "Does that mean I don't get to help out anymore? Or carry a gun?"

"Not this time, pal. But there'll be other cases."

He brightened up. "Yeah, then I can quit working at the video store."

Willie Rhoden's car pulled up, rescuing me from saying anything about the frightening idea of Deuce wielding a weapon.

"Hi Reed. Hi Deuce," she waved as she got out and locked the car door.

"Hey, Willie," Deuce hollered. "You want a Pepsi?"

She strode up the walk, looking fine even in her scrubs. "Sure. I'll take a Pepsi."

Deuce darted into the house.

"You know he has a crush on you," I said quietly.

"Uh-huh. It's cute," she said, sitting down close to me. "How are you?"

"Case closed, and I'm all in one piece," I said with a smile.

I heard the phone ring inside Deuce's place, then him talking to someone.

"Listen, about the other night," Willie said. "I got scared."

I put an arm around her, and she didn't resist. "So you still like me."

She pinched me. "I never said I didn't. I just don't want to complicate things."

"Dinner and drinks. That's not complicated."

"You know what I mean."

Deuce came back outside. "That was Bob. He's coming over for dinner, and asked if you guys would like to join us. Barbecued ribs. He makes them really good."

I raised an eyebrow at Willie. She nodded. "That sounds wonderful, Deuce."

Deuce beamed at Willie, and she beamed at me.

By the way she smiled at me, I could tell that things were looking up.

## ABOUT THE AUTHOR

Renée Pawlish is the author of The Reed Ferguson mystery series, *Nephilim Genesis of Evil, Take Five*, a short story collection that includes a Reed Ferguson mystery, and The *Sallie House: Exposing the Beast Within*, about a haunted house investigation in Kansas.

Renée loves to travel and has visited numerous countries around the world. She has also spent many summer days at her parents' cabin in the hills outside of Boulder, Colorado, which was the inspiration for the setting of Taylor Crossing in her novel *Nephilim*.

Visit Renée at www.reneepawlish.com.

**The Reed Ferguson Mystery Series**
*This Doesn't Happen In The Movies*
*Reel Estate Rip-off*

**The Nephilim Trilogy**
*Nephilim Genesis of Evil*
Books Two and Three soon to be released

**Take Five**
A Short Story Collection

**The Sallie House: Exposing the Beast Within**
Non-fiction account of a haunted house investigation in Kansas

Made in the USA
Columbia, SC
08 December 2019

84566178R00135